The Nancy Drew Files™

Carolyn Keene

The Nancy Drew Casefiles™

Secrets Can Kill

Deadly Intent

Armada

An Imprint of HarperCollins*Publishers*

Secrets Can Kill and *Deadly Intent*
were first published in the USA in 1986
by Simon and Schuster, Inc.
First published in Great Britain in Armada in 1988

First published together in this edition
in 1993 by Armada
Armada is an imprint of
HarperCollins Children's Books,
part of HarperCollins Publishers Ltd
77-85 Fulham Palace Road
Hammersmith, London W6 8JB

1 3 5 7 9 10 8 6 4 2

Copyright © 1986 Simon and Schuster

Nancy Drew and *The Nancy Drew Mystery Stories*
are registered trademarks of Simon & Schuster, Inc.

Printed and bound in Great Britain by
HarperCollins Book Manufacturing, Glasgow

Chapter

One

HANDS ON HER hips, Nancy Drew stood in the middle of her bedroom and surveyed the situation. New clothes lay everywhere—strewn across the bed, draped over the backs of chairs, and spilling out of shopping bags.

Laughing at the mess, Nancy reached for a just-bought pair of designer jeans. "How do you like the new look in private detectives?" she said, slipping the jeans on. "Undercover and overdressed!"

"I'd give anything to have a job like yours." Bess Marvin studied the label on an oversized green sweater that would be perfect with

Nancy's reddish-blond hair. "Not only did you get to buy a whole closetful of clothes for it, but you'll probably be asked out by every good-looking boy at Bedford High."

George Fayne swallowed the last of her frozen yogurt and asked, "What's going on at that school, anyway?"

"I don't know all the details yet, but it doesn't sound too terrible," Nancy said. "Lockers broken into, a few files and some video equipment missing, stuff like that." She zipped up the jeans and took the sweater Bess was holding out. "The principal, Mr. Parton, said he'd tell me more tomorrow. I won't say the case is going to be a piece of cake," Nancy said with a grin, "but it doesn't exactly sound like the hardest sleuthing I've ever done, either."

At eighteen, Nancy Drew already had a reputation in her home town of River Heights as one of the brightest, hottest young detectives around. And she'd earned every bit of that reputation the hard way—by tracking down clues and solving mysteries that ranged from arson to kidnapping.

Nancy took every case seriously, of course, but somehow, going undercover as a high-school student to find a smalltime vandal just didn't seem very heavy. After all, she'd been up against some really tough characters in the past, like armed robbers and blackmailers.

Nancy studied herself in the mirror. She liked

what she saw. The tight jeans looked great on her long, slim legs and the green sweater complemented her strawberry-blond hair. Her eyes flashed with the excitement of a new case. She was counting on solving the little mystery fairly easily. In fact, Nancy thought it would probably be fun! "Right now," she said to her two friends, "the hardest part of this case is deciding what to wear."

"That outfit, definitely," Bess said, sighing with envy at Nancy's slender figure. "You'll make the guys absolutely drool."

"That's all she needs," George joked. "A bunch of freshmen following her around like underage puppies."

"Oh, yeah? Have you seen the captain of the Bedford football team?" Bess rolled her eyes. "They don't call him 'Hunk' Hogan for nothing!"

Bess and George were Nancy's best friends, and they were cousins, but that was about all they had in common. Blond-haired Bess was bubbly and easygoing, and always on the lookout for two things: a good diet and a great date. So far she hadn't found either. She was constantly trying to lose five pounds, and she fell in and out of love every other month.

George, with curly dark hair and a shy smile, was quiet, with a dry sense of humor and the beautifully toned body of an athlete. George liked boys as much as Bess did, but she was more serious about love. "When I fall," she'd say, "it's going to be for real."

Both girls had helped Nancy to solve cases in the past, and they'd just spent the entire day with her at the shopping mall, helping Bedford High's "new girl" choose her new wardrobe.

"Anyway," Bess went on, "Nancy will be completely immune to the charms of Hunk Hogan. She's got Ned, right, Nan?"

· "Right." Nancy glanced at the mirror above her dresser, where she'd stuck a snapshot of Ned Nickerson, and her grin changed to a soft smile as she thought of the first boy she'd ever loved.

Nancy and Ned had a very special relationship. They'd known each other since they were kids, and when they'd first realized they loved each other, they'd thought it would last forever. But neither one was ready yet for a "forever" commitment, so occasionally they drifted apart, dating other people. Yet somehow, Nancy always found herself coming back to Ned. They were so in tune with each other that no matter what they were doing—whether it was tracking down the clues to a mystery or planning a private party for two—it seemed that they could read each other's thoughts.

Nancy smiled to herself and wondered if Ned knew what she was thinking at that moment, which was: that as good as he looked in a photograph, with his light brown hair, soft dark eyes, and gently curving mouth, Ned was a hundred times better in the flesh.

Shivering as she remembered the feel of his arms around her, Nancy promised herself that when she solved the Bedford High case, she would definitely join him for a long weekend with his family at their cabin in the mountains.

"You're right," she said again. "In my eyes, no guy can compete with Ned. But if I meet some really gorgeous senior, I'll be sure to get his number for you."

"Great!" Bess fingered the gold locket she always wore around her neck. When she was in love, the locket carried a picture of the lucky boy. At the moment it was empty. "But I don't want to be a complete hog," she said with a laugh. "Get a number for George, too."

George blushed and tossed a pillow at her cousin. "No, thanks. I'll find my own guy."

"I've heard that before," Bess joked. "Come on, Nancy's in a perfect position to fix us up. Who knows when we'll have a chance like this again?"

George tossed a second pillow, but by then she was laughing, too. "Nancy's supposed to be solving a crime, not setting us up."

"Who cares? She can do both! Right, Nan?"

Bess tossed one of the pillows at Nancy, Nancy tossed it back, and in a few seconds, the girls were in the middle of a full-fledged pillow fight. Soon the room was a bigger mess than ever, as feathers flew from the pillows and slowly drifted down onto the piles of clothes and shopping bags.

The free-for-all was still going strong when the Drews' housekeeper stuck her head around the door and good-naturedly dodged a flying pillow.

Hannah Gruen had been with the Drews since Nancy was born. After Mrs. Drew died, when Nancy was still a baby, Hannah's role had grown way beyond that of housekeeper. Mrs. Gruen had hugged and scolded Nancy through childhood, bandaging scraped knees and kissing away tears. As the years went by, she was always ready with encouragement and advice. And, of course, the hugging and scolding had continued, too. In time Hannah had become almost a second mother to Nancy. She was always there when Nancy's father's work as a lawyer took him away from his daughter. Carson Drew trusted Hannah implicitly, and Nancy loved her without question.

"Hannah!" Nancy giggled when she saw Mrs. Gruen in the doorway. "I know what you're going to say—it's a school night, and I'd better clean up my room fast and get to bed early!"

"Well, I couldn't help thinking that you *are* starting a new assignment tomorrow, and you *should* probably get a good night's rest," Hannah said. "But the real reason I'm here is to give you this." She handed Nancy a bulky manila envelope.

Nancy took it and saw her name printed in black marker. There was no return address, no stamp, no postmark. "Where did this come from?" she asked.

"I haven't the vaguest idea," Hannah replied. "I went out to sweep the front porch about five minutes ago and there it was, poking out of the mailbox."

Nancy fingered the package, then held it up to her ear. "Well, it's not ticking," she joked.

She ripped open the envelope and pulled out an unlabeled videotape.

"Oh, terrific," Bess said. "A movie. I've been dying to see a good movie lately."

"Too bad we don't have any popcorn," George said as they trooped down the hall toward the den.

"I just bought a bag," Hannah said, heading for the kitchen. "Come help yourselves if you get hungry."

In the den Nancy turned on the television and then opened the cabinet that held the VCR. "I wish I knew where this came from," she said. "Who goes around leaving videotapes on peoples' doorsteps?"

"Maybe it's some advertising gimmick," Bess suggested.

"No, I've got it!" George began laughing.

"It's that workout tape Bess was so interested in—the one with all the gorgeous hunks."

Nancy grinned. "Yeah, I had the feeling she was more interested in the hunks than the exercises." She slipped the tape into the deck and pushed the play button. "Okay," she said, joining Bess and George on the couch, "get ready."

The girls were still laughing as the movie started, but after the first few seconds, the laughter stopped.

"What is this, anyway?" George asked.

Leaning forward from her corner of the couch, Bess gave a little cry of surprise. "It's *us,*" she said. "Look!"

In silence the girls watched themselves doing exactly what they'd done six hours earlier: entering the shopping mall and arguing about which store to go to first.

But after that the camera stayed almost exclusively on Nancy. There she was, studying the mannequins in the window of a fashionable boutique; there she was again, coming out of a store called Ups & Downs, checking her pocketbook.

"You were afraid you'd left your credit card in the store," Bess said. "Remember?"

"I remember." Nancy didn't take her eyes off the screen. "But I don't remember anybody hanging around with a video camera, taping the whole thing."

The tape stayed on Nancy: riding the escalator, going in and out of stores, sipping a Coke. Then it showed the three friends eating hotdogs by the fountain in the center of the mall.

"It's true," Bess remarked, "the camera does add ten pounds."

George shook her head. "This has to be some kind of weird joke."

"It's weird, all right," Nancy agreed. "But if it's a joke, I'm not laughing."

"There can't be much more," Bess said. "Panache was the last store we went into."

Sure enough, as they watched themselves come out of Panache, the camera zoomed in on Nancy. The last frame froze in a close-up of her smiling face.

Nancy was reaching out to turn off the tape machine when a screeching, whining sound made her stop, her hand in midair.

Then a high-pitched, hideously shrieking voice invaded the Drews' cozy den. "Stick with shopping, Nancy Drew. It's a lot safer than snooping at Bedford High!"

Chapter

Two

EARLY THE NEXT morning, as Nancy was pulling her red Mustang out of the Drews' driveway, the sound of the frightening voice came back to her once again. "Stick to shopping, huh?" Nancy muttered under her breath. "Fat chance." She shifted her car into drive and was just stepping on the gas when she saw Hannah hurrying out the front door.

"You almost forgot this," Hannah said, handing Nancy an orange canvas duffel bag that held notebooks, pens, and makeup—everything Nancy had packed for her "first day" at school.

"Thanks, Hannah." Nancy stifled a yawn and

smiled as she took the bag. "I almost forgot my most important prop for this job."

"You don't look very alert this morning, I must say," Hannah commented. "In fact, you look downright sleepy."

"I'm fine, Hannah, really. See you later!" Nancy waved cheerfully as she drove from her house, but Hannah had been right. Nancy was definitely less than bright-eyed and bushy-tailed.

No wonder, Nancy thought. Getting to sleep the night before had been next to impossible. She was always a little edgy before she started a new case, but the past night had been worse than usual. She'd lain awake, running the mysterious videotape through her mind over and over again.

The creepiest part was that horrible voice. The sound of it had echoed in Nancy's head all night and into the morning. It had obviously been electronically distorted, but realizing that didn't make it any less scary. And knowing that someone had been following her all day was definitely frightening. Nancy couldn't help thinking about the video equipment that had been taken from Bedford High. Could there be any link between the two? Nancy wondered.

Who was responsible? And why? Why would some high school kid who was into rifling lockers and stealing a few files go to such trouble to scare her off? And how did whoever it was know about Nancy's assignment? That was the question which had kept the young detective awake the longest.

Nancy had tried not to think about those pieces to the Bedford High puzzle. She knew she wouldn't figure them out until she actually got to the school campus and did some on-the-spot research. Still, she hadn't been able to keep her mind off the troubling questions. And there she was on the first day of a case, nervous and droopy-eyed!

As she drove the fifteen miles from River Heights to the town of Bedford, Nancy tuned the car radio to her favorite rock station, hoping the music would clear her head. She slowed, passing the local Ford dealer. The new Mustang GT Convertible she'd been drooling over was still inside. *Be cool, Nancy,* she said to herself with a half-smile, trying to keep her heart from pounding. Then, pressing her foot to the accelerator, she zoomed toward town.

Bedford was beautiful, small, but with large homes surrounded by lush lawns, and, no doubt, swimming pools tucked away in the back somewhere. On the outskirts of town, along the road to the high school, Nancy passed several houses that could only be described as mansions.

Bedford was obviously a place where a lot of

rich people lived, Nancy thought as she pulled up to a stoplight near the high school. At just that moment a sleek, expensive black Porsche 911 eased up beside her in the next lane.

Nancy glanced over, admiring the car, and its owner gently revved the engine. The powerful motor gave a soft, throaty rumble, then another. Nancy smiled at the obvious come-on and lifted her gaze to the driver.

The guy in the Porsche was one of the most gorgeous boys Nancy had ever seen. He looked about seventeen. He'd probably been a tow-head when he was little, but now his blond hair was highlighted with streaks of honey-brown. And his eyes—were they brown or black?—were full of light and laughter as he gave Nancy a playful grin and revved the engine once more.

Suddenly Nancy was wide awake. She grinned back and fluttered the gas pedal on the Mustang. *Two can play this game,* she thought.

Out of the corner of her eye, Nancy saw the turn arrow change to green. Still looking at the boy, she smoothly shifted gears. Then she peeled out ahead of the Porsche, swinging wide into his lane so that he had to follow her all the way down Bedford Road. She was definitely back in high school!

Nancy lost sight of the Porsche somewhere in Bedford High's student parking lot, and as she joined the crowd of kids swarming up the school's front steps, she stopped thinking about it. Of course, its driver wasn't quite so easy to forget.

Bedford High wasn't big, with a total enrollment of about six hundred students. But it seemed to Nancy as if every one of those students was milling around in the building's big front hall. They looked like a typical bunch of kids. While they waited for the final bell, they laughed together, calling to each other, talking about dates and upcoming tests.

For a moment Nancy felt exactly like what she was pretending to be—a transfer student coming into a new school in the middle of fall semester. There she was, facing a bunch of strangers who already knew each other and were checking her out, trying to figure out who the new girl was. She felt exposed and self-conscious, and like all new kids, she wished she had a friend nearby. *That's the way you're supposed to feel*, Nancy told herself. At least it was a good cover.

Nancy was standing alone, trying to remember the directions to the principal's office that she had been given, when a snatch of conversation caught her attention.

"You know I can't give you a ride," a boy's voice said. Nancy could detect the frantic pleading in it. "I just *can't*. If I miss practice, I'll be kicked off the team!"

Then came a second boy's voice, calm and

slow and coldly self-assured. "Miss practice . . . or else," it ordered.

Nancy craned her neck, trying to locate the source of that unpleasant little exchange. There was no way, however, to match the voices to any of the faces in the mass of chattering students around her.

I guess there's at least one super-creep in every high school, Nancy thought to herself. But as she headed for the principal's office, she kept hearing the harsh sound of that calm, cold voice. There was an intimidating power in it. And obviously, whomever it belonged to had someone scared!

Nancy turned down one of Bedford High's drab green hallways. No matter how much high schools changed, she decided, the paint jobs never seemed to. Nancy found the principal's office and told the secretary that she had an appointment with Mr. Parton. The principal didn't keep Nancy waiting five seconds.

Stepping into the office, Nancy took one look at Mr. Parton and decided to try to solve this case in record time. Not only did she want that weekend with Ned, but Mr. Parton looked like he was on the verge of a nervous breakdown. For the sake of his health, she'd better work fast!

"It's driving me insane!" Mr. Parton declared, dramatically pounding his fists against his temples. "And are the police any help?

15

Noooo. Beef up security, they say. Ha! Try getting the salary for another guard out of the school board. A patrol car drives around the school every night. We can't be bothered with a little file-filching. It's your problem, they say."

Mr. Parton paused for breath and then chuckled to himself, shaking his bald head and smiling at Nancy with worried brown eyes. "Thank heavens I know your father. If he hadn't suggested that I hire you, I don't know what I'd have done."

Probably collapsed, Nancy told herself, but she kept her thoughts silent. She smiled. "I'm glad you did call me, Mr. Parton. I'm ready to get started, but first I just want to make sure I've got the facts straight. You mentioned files being taken. What files?"

"Actually, we're not sure." Mr. Parton shook his head again. "But my file cabinet and the senior guidance counselor's—both of which are kept locked, by the way—have been tampered with several times. We don't know if anything's missing because everything's always put back in the wrong place.

"Then there are the lockers," Mr. Parton went on, rubbing one hand over his shiny head. "We know that at least four lockers have been broken into. Our maintenance man reported them." He leaned forward, hands clasped. "But no students complained."

"It could have something to do with drugs,"

Nancy suggested. "That would explain why the kids kept their mouths shut."

"True. And I won't say that Bedford High is drug-free. But I do know for sure that there aren't any drugs in my file cabinet. And what about the school video equipment?"

Right, Nancy thought, remembering the "movie" she'd received.

"Whoever's taking the stuff is very selective," the principal said. "We lose a lens here, a battery pack there, then a couple of blank tapes. Some of it's even turned up mysteriously a few days after disappearing."

"And you're sure whoever's pulling all these stunts is one person?" Nancy asked.

"I'm not sure of anything," Mr. Parton said, frustration mounting in his voice. "But I'm almost certain that a student, or more than one student, is behind it all."

"Why couldn't it be a teacher?"

"Well, the police, much as I'm disappointed in them, did do me one favor. They questioned the faculty, checked them out, and came up with zilch, except for the bio teacher, who turned out to be a scofflaw. Two hundred dollars in unpaid parking tickets."

Nancy laughed. "Well, having me pose as a student was a good idea." She stood up and reached for her canvas bag. "I'd like to get started, but first I need to know if I have your permission to check things out my own way. I mean, I may have to break a few rules to get to the bottom of this."

"Whatever it takes. I'll clear it with the police," Mr. Parton said emphatically. "And don't go yet." He motioned for Nancy to sit again. "I may not be thinking too clearly these days, but I do know that you'll need a contact while you're here, somebody you can talk to freely. Someone who can introduce you to a lot of kids. The principal isn't going to help any student fit in. Even I know that."

"Your thinking's not all that fuzzy, Mr. Parton." Nancy laughed again. "So. Who's my contact?"

"One of our seniors. A good student, completely trustworthy. And very popular, president of the class, which is why I chose him. He can get you in touch with all the various 'crowds.'"

"You mean he knows about me already?" Nancy asked, once again thinking about the videotape.

"No, I thought I'd introduce you two and let him in on the plan at the same time." Mr. Parton checked his watch. "He should be here any minute."

At that moment there was a knock at the door. Mr. Parton opened it, and Nancy looked up and found herself face to face with the beautiful driver of the black Porsche!

"Nancy Drew," the principal said, "meet Daryl Gray."

His eyes weren't brown or black, Nancy noticed immediately. They were the dark, dusky color of ripe blueberries, and they were rimmed with lashes that had to be at least half an inch long. Nancy had never seen eyes like that in her life.

Some contact! she thought.

Daryl Gray listened politely and with interest as Mr. Parton explained the entire situation. If he was surprised at Nancy's role, he didn't show it.

Instead, Daryl's incredible eyes kept straying to Nancy each time Mr. Parton mentioned her name. And when the principal said something about Daryl showing Nancy the ropes, Daryl's mouth curved into a slow, teasing grin. Nancy couldn't help returning it.

The attraction between them crackled like electricity. Nancy wondered how Mr. Parton could possibly miss the sparks, but he seemed oblivious to everything but his problem. He went on and on. As Nancy tuned out the principal's voice, she tuned into the beautiful face before her.

Finally the harried principal said something that brought Nancy back to reality. "Nancy, the school is counting on you. I've done what I can. Now it's up to you. At this moment Daryl is the only one, aside from me, who knows who you are and what you're doing here. The rest is in your hands."

And Nancy, remembering that hideous voice on the tape, finally tore her eyes away from Daryl. *You're wrong, Mr. Parton,* she thought. *Somebody else knows who I am. And that's the person I have to find!*

Chapter
Three

THE WARNING BELL rang just as Nancy and Daryl left Mr. Parton's office. Together they fell into step with the crowd of kids hurrying to their homeroom classes. Out of the corner of her eye Nancy caught Daryl looking at her, a strange little smile on his lips. "What's funny?" she asked.

"Nothing." Daryl laughed softly and shook his head. "It's just that I've never met a detective, especially a beautiful redhead who drives a Mustang."

Nancy laughed too. "Well, I've never met a senior who drives a Porsche."

"It's my favorite toy." They rounded a corner

and Daryl casually put his hand on Nancy's shoulder to guide her out of the way of a group of kids coming in the opposite direction. "I'll have to give you a ride sometime, show you what it can do."

At the touch of Daryl's hand, Nancy felt a delicious tingling sensation, and suddenly she found herself wondering what it would be like to have Daryl's arms around her. Daryl Gray was a powerfully attractive guy.

"Do you think it would be good for making fast getaways?" Nancy went on in the same teasing manner.

"Sure," Daryl replied, leaving his hand where it was, "but I hope you're not planning to make a getaway real soon. After all, we just met."

"And besides, I have a mystery to solve, remember?"

"Right. And I hope it takes a long, long time."

They were both laughing, looking into each other's eyes as they turned another corner and bumped into what felt to Nancy like a rock wall.

"Sorry," the wall said.

Nancy touched her nose to make sure it wasn't broken, and then smiled at the guy, who was big and handsome, and built like a truck.

"Walt, meet Nancy Drew. She's a transfer student," Daryl said smoothly. "Nancy, Walt Hogan."

Nancy smiled again, remembering what Bess had said about Bedford's football captain. "Hunk" fit him perfectly.

"Yeah," Walt said, not returning her smile, "nice to meet you."

Walt strode off, and Nancy turned to Daryl. "He seemed a little angry," she commented.

"Yeah, he hasn't been Mr. Friendly lately," Daryl agreed. "And you should see him in action on the field. He's like a bear just out of hibernation—mean and hungry."

"I don't suppose he's a video freak, by any chance?"

"I thought detectives were supposed to be more subtle than that."

"Why should I be subtle with you?" Nancy teased. "You're my contact, aren't you?"

Daryl's hand tightened on Nancy's shoulder. "I sure am," he said softly.

Nancy and Daryl were standing in front of Nancy's homeroom class, waiting for the final bell to ring. About ten other kids were waiting, too, and as Nancy laughed at Daryl's last remark, she caught a girl staring at them.

The girl was blond, pretty in a tough, hard-edged kind of way, but she didn't look too friendly, Nancy thought. She was watching Daryl intently. Then as someone called out "Carla!" she moved her eyes to Nancy's face for just a second before turning away. In that brief instant she gave Nancy the strangest look. It wasn't a look of dislike, Nancy thought, it was more like a challenge. She wondered how much this Carla knew about her.

The final bell rang, and Daryl gave Nancy's shoulder another squeeze. "I guess this is it for now," he said. He leaned so close that Nancy felt his breath on her ear. "You're on your own, detective."

Actually, Nancy didn't expect to do much detecting on her first day. She was new in school; she had to find her way around, get used to the rhythm of the place, and meet a few people before she could start asking questions.

Part of Nancy's cover was to act like a new girl—lost and a little out of it—which was easy, since that was how she felt. Daryl wasn't in any of her classes and she didn't know anyone else.

Most of the kids ignored Nancy. The first really friendly girl she met was a pretty blond with aquamarine eyes, who waylaid Nancy after English.

"Hi, I'm Sara Ames," she said. "You're new here, aren't you?"

"My name's Nancy Drew, and you're right, I'm brand-new."

"Well, don't worry, you'll fit in fast," Sara said. "But I wanted to get to you before anybody else did."

"Oh?" Nancy wondered if Sara might have some secret information.

"I'm editor of the *Bedford Sentinel*," Sara went on, "and we're desperate for people to work on the paper. I noticed in English that you can at least read and write," she joked. "And I bet you're going to be popular, so you'll have lots of good contacts. The *Sentinel*'s fun. What do you think?"

Nancy smiled to herself at the thought of her "contact." She smiled at Sara, too, for making her feel welcomed. "Thanks for asking," she said. "Let me feel my way around a little more, okay? Then I'll let you know."

"Great! There's a staff meeting tonight, room 215. I hope you can make it." With a friendly wave, Sara dashed down the hall.

Nancy's next class was American history. She'd almost forgotten just how boring a bad teacher could be, but the droning voice, the intimidating looks, all of it reminded her why she'd been happy to leave high school behind. She'd certainly be happy to leave history behind! The forty-five minute period dragged on and on. Halfway through, Nancy let her mind wander. Anything was better than the teacher's monotone!

Purposely putting Bedford High's mystery out of her mind, Nancy thought about Sara Ames's offer to join the newspaper staff. She was tempted to accept it. Maybe she could have a double cover—new girl and student reporter, investigating the vandal of Bedford High. It might work, she thought. But once she solved the case, she'd be leaving the school, and that would leave Sara minus one reporter. It didn't seem fair.

When American history was finally over, Nancy heaved a sigh of relief along with the rest of the students. "Class," the teacher called over the noise of the final bell, "read the next two chapters in your textbook for homework."

"Great," Nancy groaned to herself. "Boring homework, too." The Bedford High mystery was turning out to have hidden liabilities!

On the way to lunch Nancy spotted Sara Ames at the entrance to the cafeteria and decided to tell her she wouldn't be joining the newspaper. That way Sara wouldn't feel hurt when Nancy didn't show up at the staff meeting.

"Hi," Nancy said. "Listen, thanks for asking me to join the paper, but I think I'd better make sure my grades are in good enough shape before I do anything else, you know?"

"Okay," said Sara. "I understand. Just let me know whenever you're ready."

"Thanks," said Nancy.

Sara rushed off, and Nancy entered the cafeteria. She looked around uncertainly. Where should she sit?

At that moment she heard someone call her name. Turning, she saw Connie Watson waiting in the cafeteria line.

Nancy knew Connie's name because the

teacher had called on her in French class. Connie's face had turned the color of a ripe tomato as she'd given her answer, and after class Nancy had noticed that no one walked out of the room with her. Connie was slightly pudgy, but her eyes, though anxious and a little fearful, were friendly. She smiled shyly and said, "Hey, would you like to eat lunch with me?"

"I wish I could," Nancy said sincerely, "but I've got to talk to the counselor about my schedule—I've been stuck with two gym classes, can you believe it? I'm just going to grab a yogurt and keep going!"

What Nancy really wanted was a chance to snoop around the video lab, providing it was empty. If it wasn't, maybe she could ask a few "innocent" questions.

After promising Connie that she'd sit with her the next day, Nancy paid for her yogurt, headed down the hall, turned a corner, and stopped. *Some detective you are,* she told herself. *You didn't even bother to find out where the video lab is!*

Nancy was about ready to go back to the cafeteria and ask Connie when she saw Carla walking toward her. Nancy hadn't forgotten the challenging look Carla had given her that morning, but she put on a bright smile anyway. "Hi. This is embarrassing, but I'm lost. Could you point me in the direction of the video lab?"

"Oh, it's easy to get lost in this place," Carla said with a friendly smile. "Just go to the end of this hall, turn left and follow the hall to the end. Then go through the door on your right and down the stairs. You can't miss it."

"Thanks," Nancy said, just as nicely. "I appreciate it."

Maybe I was just being paranoid this morning, she thought as she walked along. Nancy turned left and went down the second hall. She pushed open the door, started down the steps, and stopped. The staircase obviously wasn't going to take her to the video lab. From the look of things, it would probably lead straight to the boiler room.

On the other hand, she thought, *maybe Carla really is a prime pain in the you-know-what.*

Or maybe Carla had something to do with the anonymous videotape. That might explain why she would go out of her way to steer Nancy away from the video lab.

Nancy was moving back up the stairs when she heard scuffling sounds from below. She stopped, listening, then heard a muffled shout.

"Just lay off, Jake," a voice said. "I've given you what you want, so get off my back." The voice grew angrier. "You're a nobody, Webb, a real waste of space. Why don't you make like a ghost and vanish?"

Footsteps pounded up the stairs. Before Nancy could move, Walt Hogan, the surly star of the football team, was beside her. He wasn't just surly, though. He was furious, his face flushed with anger. Walt shouldered Nancy roughly aside. Then his fury exploded and he rammed his clenched fists into the door before shoving it open and storming through.

While Nancy tried to decide whether to run after Walt, she heard a soft laugh. Looking down, she saw another boy, one she hadn't met before, staring up at her.

"Well, if it isn't Bedford High's newest scholar, Nancy Drew," the boy sneered. "I'm Jake Webb."

Jake smiled as he began climbing the stairs toward Nancy, but the look in his eyes was cold. "Do you always go around poking your nose into other people's business?" he asked. "Not too nice, Nancy Drew. Maybe I ought to explain a few rules to you. Otherwise, you won't get very far at Bedford High."

Nancy recognized the voice. It was the same one she'd heard in the main hall that morning, coolly ordering some desperate kid to "miss practice—or else." Jake's face went with his voice, Nancy thought—lean and bony, with a tight-lipped smile under sharp, ice-blue eyes.

Nancy felt an overwhelming urge to tell the creep to buzz off. But Jake wasn't acting like the average high-school egomaniac, and she was curious to see what he was up to.

Jake climbed the stairs until his eyes were

level with Nancy's. Still smiling, he ran one finger lazily up her arm, across her neck, and to her lips.

"Rule One," Jake said softly. "Keep your mouth shut about what you just heard. If you don't, you'll never learn Rule Two."

Chapter

Four

NANCY WAS TEMPTED to bite Jake's finger and see what happened, but instead she forced herself to push his hand away calmly. She was so furious, she didn't even think about being frightened. Who did this guy think he was, anyway?

"Who makes these rules?" she asked. "You, I suppose?"

"Clever Nancy," Jake said with a laugh. "Go to the head of the class."

The longer Nancy stood there, the stronger the urge she had to push Jake Webb down the stairs. She'd already decided that he was a prime candidate for the Bedford High vandal (not to mention the Bedford town jail), but at the moment all she wanted was to get rid of him.

"Look," she said, "I don't know what you're trying to do, but I think I ought to tell you that I don't scare easily." She put her hand on the door. "Why don't you just crawl back under your rock?"

Without waiting for Jake's reaction, Nancy pulled the door open and almost bumped into Daryl Gray.

"Well, well," Jake scoffed. "It's 'King Cool.'"

Completely ignoring Jake, Daryl smiled at Nancy. "Hi. I expected to see you in the cafeteria."

"She couldn't make it," Jake said. "She had more important things to do than eat."

"You okay?" Daryl asked Nancy.

"I was getting a little bored with the company, but I'm fine now," she said. "How'd you know I was here?"

"Are you kidding?" Jake leaned against the doorjamb and grinned. "King Cool has the inside track on everything—girls, cars, clever ways to make money. Right, King?"

Quickly Daryl shifted his glance to Jake. "You talk too much, Webb," he said sharply. "I'm tired of the sound of your voice. Do everybody a favor and give your mouth a rest."

"Anything you say, King." Jake held Daryl's

gaze for a second. "But my eyes'll still be open—you can count on that." Then he slouched off down the hall.

Nancy let out her breath. "What was all that business about your money and keeping his eyes open?"

"Hard to tell with that guy," Daryl said. "How'd you run into him, anyway?"

Nancy explained, and noticed a funny look on Daryl's face when she mentioned Carla, but she decided not to ask about it. "Anyway, I'm glad you came along," she said. "I was just about ready to blow my cover with that creep."

"Jake Webb's personality fits his name," Daryl said with a grimace. "He's just like a spider waiting for a fly to come along. I can't believe he actually works in the principal's office. But most of us here aren't candidates for the psycho ward like he is. I'll prove it to you if you'll come to the dance with me this week-end."

"That's a pretty intriguing invitation," Nancy said with a coy smile. "I'm too curious to turn you down."

"It's a date, then."

Daryl touched her arm in a familiar gesture before walking away. Once again, Nancy thrilled to the feel of his hand. As she hurried to her next class, she pictured the two of them dancing together, arms around each other. The picture brought a smile to her face. As long as she was at Bedford High, she thought, she might as well have some fun. And Daryl Gray was the perfect person to have it with.

By the time her last class of the day was over, Nancy's head was a blur of names and faces, a jumble of bells and pounding feet. As she'd expected, she hadn't done much detecting at all. Only two people—Carla and Jake—stood out in her mind as possibly connected to the vandalism and to the videotape she'd received.

She wanted to find out more about both of them, but first she wanted to take a look around the video lab to see if she could discover any connection between the missing equipment and the mysterious tape.

She wasn't taking any chances on getting lost a second time—she asked a teacher for directions and, after stashing some books in her locker, made her way to room 235.

The door was locked. *Probably only the teacher has a key.* Well, Mr. Parton *had* given her permission to do "whatever it takes," she thought. She reached into her duffel bag and pulled out an extremely handy little device—a credit card—and took a careful look down the hall.

Connie Watson was walking straight toward her.

"Hi, Nancy!" Connie called. "I've been looking for you. The football team's got practice this afternoon and I thought you might want to go to it with me." Connie blushed and bit her lip. "You don't have to, though. I mean, if you're too busy, that's okay," she said quickly, as if she were used to being rejected.

"No, I think I'd like that," Nancy said, pocketing the credit card. Maybe she'd get a chance to talk to Walt Hogan. She was very curious about the cryptic conversation she'd overheard on the stairs. "Let's go."

The weather was warm for early October, and several dozen kids were sitting in the bleachers watching the players and the cheerleading squad. Nancy and Connie arrived just in time to see Hunk Hogan getting chewed out royally by the coach. Nancy couldn't hear what was being said, but she wondered if Walt was in trouble because he'd arrived late. If that was it, then it was probably his voice she'd heard in the main hall that morning, pleading with Jake. She hadn't recognized it when she met him, but if it *was* Walt, then she had more reason than ever to talk to him.

The cheerleaders were energetic and colorful in their bright orange and white uniforms. Nancy admired their routines and even had to admit that Carla, who seemed to be the captain, was very good.

Beside her, Connie sighed. "I'd give anything

to be a cheerleader," she confided. "Of course, I'm too fat, so it's not worth thinking about. Besides, even if I were skinny, I'd never make it. Not with Carla Dalton in charge. She can't stand me."

Nancy nodded sympathetically. "She's not too crazy about me, either, but I don't have a clue why."

"Oh, that's easy," Connie said. "Ever since you arrived at Bedford High, Daryl Gray hasn't taken his eyes off of you, and Carla can't stand competition." She put her hand over her mouth and giggled. "Personally, I love seeing Carla get what she deserves."

"You mean Carla and Daryl have a thing going?" Nancy asked. That explained the funny look on Daryl's face when Carla's name had been mentioned. Nancy couldn't picture Daryl being interested in someone like that, but she really didn't know him all that well.

"Off and on," Connie told her. "It's been off for a couple of weeks, but when you showed up, I guess Carla decided you were invading her territory."

So Carla's jealous, Nancy thought. That might make her nasty, but it didn't make her a criminal.

"Actually, I'm surprised she still wants Daryl," Connie went on. "Carla's only interested in one thing—money."

"Well, Daryl can't be heading for the poorhouse," Nancy remarked. "Not if he drives around in a Porsche."

"It is a little weird," Connie agreed, "especially since his father lost practically all his money a few months ago in some big business fiasco. For a while the Grays were one of the richest families in Bedford, but now . . ."

Connie's voice trailed off as she shook her head in sympathy. Nancy was sympathetic, too, but she was also curious. Not about the Grays' money problems—that was simply none of her business—but about what other tidbits of information Connie might have. She was something of a gossip, Nancy thought, and gossips could be a big help. Connie was chattering away again, pointing out various kids on the field, when Nancy noticed the bracelet on her right wrist. "That's beautiful," she said, touching it. "What is it, art deco?"

"I . . . I don't know," Connie said nervously fingering the intricately patterned gold. "It was a present . . . I don't know anything about jewelry."

"I love it. It looks like an antique," Nancy told her. A little flattery never hurt when you wanted information, and besides, she really liked Connie. "So, tell me more about Bedford High," she prompted. "Hey, I hear there're some weird things going on—stuff getting stolen and lockers broken into."

"You must mean the 'phantom,'" Connie

said, seeming relieved at the change in subject. "That's what I call him, since no one knows who he is."

"Got any ideas?"

"No. And most kids don't really care. I mean, it's all so juvenile."

So much for inside information. Then Nancy had to sit on the hard bleachers for an hour as Connie proceeded to give her a detailed account of everyone's love life, grades, family, and friends. Nancy learned a lot, but nothing that was going to help. One day down, she thought. How many more to go?

Nancy arrived at school the next day, determined to start putting the puzzle together, or at least to gather a few of the pieces.

Instead of study hall she had gym during second period, and stretching her muscles and limbering up felt good. Maybe the exercise would limber her mind up, too, so she could solve the case.

Two minutes into gym, though, her mind was on something else.

"Excuse me," a voice said.

Nancy stopped in the middle of a sit-up and smiled at Carla Dalton, who was standing over her. Who knows, she thought, maybe a smile would help.

"I'd really appreciate it," Carla said, "if you'd keep your problems to yourself."

"What are you talking about?"

Carla put a hand on her cocked hip. "I'm talking about the way you ran and tattled to Daryl yesterday," she said nastily. "He chewed me out about it this morning. I mean, can't you fight your own battles?"

"Let's get something straight," Nancy said calmly. "I didn't 'tattle' to Daryl. He asked me how I got lost, and I told him. I don't want to fight with you, Carla," she went on, "but since you asked, yes, I can fight my own battles—and I usually win."

Nancy went back to her sit-ups, still smiling, but inside she was seething. *This is all I need,* she thought, *a cat fight.*

A few minutes later, though, she wondered just how petty the cat fight was going to be. It was her turn on the trampoline, and as she prepared to go into a high flip, she noticed that the girl spotting her had changed places—with Carla Dalton.

It threw her concentration off. It shouldn't have, but it did. And as she sprung high into the air, she knew she was off balance.

There was no time to catch herself. If she'd had a reliable person spotting her, she wouldn't have worried, but Carla's back, she noticed, was conveniently turned. Before Nancy could stop herself, she was hurtling over the end of the trampoline—heading for a major collision with the floor!

Chapter

Five

At the last possible second, Nancy pushed her body to the limit, twisted desperately in midair, and hit the floor—with her rear end. Thank goodness not with her head. It wasn't the most graceful move she'd ever made, but as she sat there breathing shakily, she decided that it was better to be a klutz than a corpse.

Nancy was tempted to prove to Carla then and there that she was ready to fight the battle. But when she got to her feet, she noticed that the gym teacher was doing it for her.

"Dalton!" Miss Gibbs was livid. "This isn't the pom-pom squad. You have to use your brains in here, if you have any! Drew could have broken her neck!"

Which would not have broken Carla's heart, Nancy thought grimly. It would have made her day.

Most of the girls had rushed over to Nancy, asking if she was all right, whether she needed to see the nurse, whether she was sure nothing was broken.

"Thanks," Nancy said gratefully. "I'm still in one piece. But I think I lost something."

"What?" somebody asked.

"An inch off my hips," Nancy joked. "It's permanently embedded in the gym floor!"

Twenty minutes later, Nancy took her seat in social studies. She was still slightly rattled and was hoping for a lecture so she could just take notes and get her breath back.

"Okay," the teacher said gleefully, "clear your desks of everything but paper and pen. It's pop-quiz time!"

Nancy joined the other kids in groaning, and took as long as possible finding a notebook and pen.

"Don't worry," the boy behind her said. "Mr. Warner's quizzes are so bad, nobody passes. If you flunk, you won't be alone."

"Right," the girl to her left said. "The only one with a chance is Hal Morgan."

Nancy glanced to her right and noticed that

Hal Morgan was chewing his fingernails nervously.

"He doesn't look too confident," she whispered.

"Yeah, that's weird," the girl whispered back. "You know, it's funny. Hal's been the class brain forever. Always studying, you know? Never had time for anything else. But then this September, he surprised everybody by running for class president against Daryl Gray. He didn't win, but he sure did try. I can't believe how much time he spent campaigning."

"Maybe that's why he looks nervous," Nancy said. "Maybe his grades dropped during the campaign."

The girl shrugged. "Maybe. But he's been talking about going to Harvard, so he must be doing something right. And his SATs were off the top of the scale."

"Okay, scholars," Mr. Warner cackled. "Let's get this show on the road!"

By the fifth question, Nancy had decided that the boy behind her was right. There was no way she was going to pass the quiz. At least she didn't have to worry about her grade-point average, like everybody else.

She glanced at the clock, to see how much more torture she might have to go through. As she did she noticed that Hal Morgan seemed to be having trouble concentrating, too. In fact, his eyes were on *Nancy's* paper. As soon as he saw her glance at him, he looked away.

The teacher asked the next question, and Nancy wrote down her answer. Then she deliberately put her hands to her hair so her paper would be clear.

Sure enough, Hal made a pretense of stretching and yawning, and as he rolled his head around, his eyes once more zeroed in on Nancy's paper.

It was obvious, to Nancy anyway, that Hal the Brain was copying her answers. But why? Why would somebody so smart bother to cheat on a pop quiz?

Well, it sure isn't going to do him any good, she thought as they passed their papers to the front. *Hal's going to get exactly what I get, which is probably a fifty.*

She didn't think much more of the incident until after class. As she left the room, she saw Jake Webb lurking in the hall. Then she saw Hal walk up to him, reluctantly, the way most people walk into a dentist's office.

Wondering what those two could possibly have in common, Nancy attached herself to a group of kids who were standing around, moaning about the quiz.

It was hard to hear everything, but she caught enough to make her extremely curious.

"Listen," Hal was saying, "I've got my own essay to write before I can get to yours!"

"That's cool," Jake said. "I'll give you till tomorrow. How's that?"

"That's not enough time, and you know it." Hal sounded panicky.

"Oh, too bad," said Jake sarcastically. "Well, I guess I don't have to tell you what'll happen, right?"

Hal let out a big sigh and Nancy saw the defeated look on his face. "Okay, okay," he said. "You'll have it tomorrow."

That guy is really the pits, Nancy thought as she watched Jake walk cockily down the hall. *He acts like a king, and he's got at least two lackeys—Walt and Hal—doing his bidding. How many others are hustling to follow his orders? And why? Why would anyone want to do anything for Jake Webb?*

Without really thinking about it, Nancy had begun following Jake, but when she saw him turn into another hall and open his locker, she decided she might learn something about him if she could see what was inside that locker. She didn't know what she'd be looking for—money, maybe—but it was worth a try.

As she passed him she got a look at the locker number—515—and before Jake saw her, she walked quickly to the water fountain at the end of the hall. She had to drink enough to float a ship, but finally she saw Jake's scuffed sneakers pass by and out of sight.

It was lunch time and the hall was empty.

Nancy moved quickly to locker 515. A credit card wouldn't be any help this time. But a professional lock-picker's kit would. Fortunately, along with her makeup and lunch money, Nancy's canvas bag just happened to have such a kit. She found the right-size pick and had the padlock off in half a minute. She pulled the door open and was ready for a leisurely exploration when she heard a voice.

"Be back in a second," it said, "I forgot my psych book."

It was Jake Webb. Quickly Nancy raked her eyes over the inside of his locker. Only one thing caught her attention—a shoebox. Dangling from it was a beautiful gold bracelet, *exactly* like Connie Watson's.

That was all Nancy had time for. She shut the door and moved away just as she heard Jake's footsteps round the corner.

He has no way of knowing what you were up to, she told herself. *Just keep on going.*

Nancy kept on going, but she was sure Jake Webb's eyes were on her back every step of the way.

She was glad to get out of his sight, even though once she was, Nancy still couldn't relax. What was Connie's bracelet doing in a shoebox in Jake Webb's locker? It had to be the same bracelet; it was an antique, probably one of a kind. Maybe Connie lost it and Jake, lowlife that he was, found it and decided to stash it.

When Nancy spotted Connie in the lunch line she decided to make sure she was right. "Hi," she said. "Guess what? I think I know where your bracelet is!"

Connie jumped as if she'd been stung. "My—my bracelet?"

Nancy pointed to Connie's bare wrist. "Right. You lost it, didn't you?"

Connie nodded, her eyes wide.

"Well," Nancy went on, "I'm pretty sure I saw it—are you ready?—in Jake Webb's locker!"

Shaking her head, Connie backed away slowly, fear in her eyes. "It—it couldn't be mine," she stammered. "I lost mine at home. I mean, I didn't lose it. I just didn't wear it today, that's all."

"Connie, what's wrong?"

"Nothing!" the frightened girl said. "Really, nothing's wrong! I have to go. There's this meeting I forgot about. I have to go," she said again, and all but ran away.

Some really weird things are going on at Bedford High, Nancy thought as she watched Connie hurry off. *And so far, they all lead to one person—Jake Webb.* She didn't know if Jake was the phantom vandal, or the anonymous videotaper. But she did know he was up to something. All she had to do was find out what.

* * *

By the end of the day Nancy was ready to explode. First Connie had treated her as if she had some horrible communicable disease. Then she couldn't find Walt Hogan or Hal Morgan, so she hadn't been able to question them. Plus, her rear end still ached from that fall off the trampoline. Things were definitely not going well. What she wanted most of all was to go home and soak in a hot tub.

Instead, Nancy decided she'd better make another pass at the video lab. She didn't want to leave Bedford High empty-handed, not for the second day in a row.

The lab wasn't locked. When Nancy walked in, the only person there was Daryl Gray, who was peering at a shelf of tapes. Suddenly she felt happy for the first time all day.

"Am I glad to see you!" she cried.

Daryl spun around, startled. Then his lips parted in his Porsche-driver's grin. "Nancy Drew, isn't it? New girl and"—he glanced around at the otherwise empty room—"private eye? How's the detecting going?"

"Don't ask," Nancy said with a groan. "Anyway, what are you doing here? I didn't know you belonged to the video club."

"I don't," Daryl said. "I was just doing some detecting of my own—looking for you." He came to stand within hugging distance of Nancy. "Looks like we found each other."

The nearness of him made Nancy forget all her problems. "I'm glad we did," she said. "I'm so glad, in fact, that I'm inviting you to go for a Coke. Right now."

"Sounds great to me."

"Good. I'll drive," Nancy said teasingly, "and let you see what my Mustang can do."

As they walked through the parking lot, Nancy spotted Jake Webb among the cars. Probably siphoning gas, she thought. Every time she saw him, she remembered how he'd threatened her on the stairs the day before. Was that his first threat? Or had he tried to scare her off before with the videotape?

Then Daryl put his hand casually on Nancy's shoulder and she forgot about Jake Webb and simply enjoyed the touch of Daryl Gray.

"How is it going, really?" Daryl asked again as they got into the Mustang. "Have you found any clues? Are any of the pieces fitting together yet?"

Nancy started the car with a roar. "I never thought I'd say this," she admitted with a wry smile, "but right now, the last thing on earth I want to do is solve a mystery."

Glad to be leaving, Nancy headed out of the parking lot and down Bedford Road. Daryl didn't ask any more questions about the case, and she was grateful. There'd be plenty of time to think about it later; just then, all she wanted to do was drive.

As they headed away from the high school, Bedford Road became narrow and winding. Through the trees Nancy caught glimpses of water.

"That's Bedford Lake," Daryl pointed out. "It has some nice secluded benches. Why don't you drive down there?"

Down is right, Nancy thought as the grade suddenly became steeper. She'd been doing about thirty-five and all of a sudden the needle climbed to fifty. A blind curve was coming up. Nancy put her foot on the brake. The pedal sank to the floor, and her stomach sank with it.

"Hey," Daryl said, "I don't want to sound like a driver's ed teacher, but don't you think you should slow down a little?"

Nancy couldn't answer him. The brakes were gone, and her car was shooting down the winding road, completely out of control!

Chapter

Six

THE CAR PICKED up speed, careening wildly down the hill. Nancy downshifted to second, then to first. The Mustang slowed, but not enough.

"Sharp curve coming up." Daryl spoke quietly, but Nancy heard the quiver in his voice. She couldn't blame him—she was too terrified to speak.

Hands glued to the wheel, Nancy guided the car into the curve, praying that she wouldn't meet another car coming up. The road remained clear, but it also grew steeper. And as she came out of the bend, she could see the stop sign at the bottom of the hill. It was still fifty yards away, but in her imagination she was already on top of it, could see the Mustang tearing into the intersection and colliding with whoever was unlucky enough to be in the wrong place at the wrong time.

Amazed that her hand was steady, Nancy reached over and slowly pulled up the handbrake. It didn't work. The car was going so fast that the brakes had burned out.

The stop sign was looming up like a monster's claw in a 3-D movie. There was no time to think. Instinctively Nancy aimed her car at the soft shoulder on the opposite side of the road. With an impact that snapped their heads back, the Mustang hit the bank, went up on two wheels, and wobbled for what seemed like an eternity. But finally, with a bone-jarring thump, it landed upright.

Nancy shut her eyes and leaned her head on the steering wheel. She was breathing like a marathon runner. When she opened her eyes again, she saw Daryl pry his hand loose from the dashboard. "Well," he said with a gasp, "so that's what your Mustang can do."

Nancy reached for his hand and held on tight. She felt like crying, but when she opened her mouth, a giggle came out. It was a perfectly normal hysterical reaction, she told herself. Then she giggled again.

There was a smile in Daryl's voice as he said, "How about letting me in on the joke?"

"It's just"—Nancy tried to stop laughing and couldn't—"I remembered that my car is due for an inspection in two weeks. Now the gears are probably stripped, the front bumper has to be completely smashed, and the brakes are burned out—" This last thought brought Nancy out of her dreamworld.

Her car! What had gone wrong? True, it needed an inspection, but that was just an official thing. Besides, she'd had new brakes installed six weeks ago. Something awfully strange was going on, and whatever it was, Nancy had a definite feeling that it wasn't good. She pushed open the door and jumped out.

"Hey! Where're you going?" Daryl called, rolling down his window. He stuck his head out and saw Nancy kneeling by the left front wheel, peering underneath the fender. "What is it?" he asked.

Nancy stood up, so angry she could hardly see straight. "The brake cable," she said grimly. "It's been cut."

"What?! Are you sure? I don't get it. Who'd . . . ?"

"Wait!" Nancy held her hand up for quiet. Then she sniffed the air. Frowning, she ran to the back of the car and sniffed again.

"What's wrong now?!"

Nancy could hardly believe what she was going to say. "That rock we went over? I think it cracked the gas tank. Daryl, the car could blow! It could blow any second!" She started down the hill. "Get out of the car. Hurry up!"

There were no footsteps behind her. "Nancy!" she heard Daryl call. "Nancy, I can't open the door! It's jammed!"

Nancy didn't hesitate. She raced back to the car and fought with the door from the outside, but she couldn't get a good grip on the handle because the door was on an angle, leaning toward her.

She ran to the driver's side. The smell of gas fumes was stronger than ever.

"Get your seat belt off," she said to Daryl, finally managing to open her door. She helped him climb out. "Now let's *go!*" She grabbed his hand. "The car's already beginning to burn!" she said as they ran desperately down the hill.

When the car blew, they were only a few yards away from it. The force of the explosion flung them into the underbrush by the side of the road.

They clung to each other. For a moment, hardly able to speak, they stared at the burning sportscar.

"Nancy, are you all right?" Daryl whispered at last. His eyes were bright with concern.

Nancy nodded. Feeling the heat of Daryl's breath against her cheek, she hardly noticed her bruised knee and scratched arms. It seemed the most natural thing in the world for them to keep their arms around each other. Nancy closed her eyes and breathed deeply. When Daryl had first touched her two days before, in the hallway, she'd wondered what his arms would feel like. Now she knew—they felt fabulous.

But with that fabulous feeling came another feeling—guilt. It wasn't Ned whose arms were holding her; it wasn't Ned whose lips she was feeling, nor Ned whose voice was murmuring her name. And hadn't she said just three days before that nobody could compete with Ned Nickerson? Well, maybe no one could in the long run. But at the moment—in the short run—Daryl Gray was doing a pretty good job of it.

It was a dangerous moment, emotionally, and Nancy knew she wasn't ready to deal with it. Before Daryl's lips reached hers again, she eased herself gently from his arms.

"Hey," she said softly.

"Hey, yourself." Daryl's blue eyes were smiling. Looking at Nancy, he gave a long sigh. "So," he said in a throaty voice, "how about answering the question I never got a chance to ask. Who would do something crazy like this?"

"I have a pretty good idea." Anger made Nancy's voice tight. She pulled away and felt herself stiffen. "Does the name Jake Webb ring any bells?"

"Jake? Sure," Daryl said slowly, sitting up. "I can see him doing something like this. But there's no way you can prove it, is there?"

Nancy was silent for a moment. She was remembering Jake's threat on the stairs, remembering him in the parking lot half an hour ago, hearing that voice on the videotape: "Stick with shopping, Nancy Drew. It's a lot safer than snooping at Bedford High."

Well, she hadn't done much "snooping" yet, but she hadn't backed off either. Had Jake, for some reason, decided to stop her before she got any further?

"You're right," she said as she and Daryl got up and brushed the leaves and dirt off their clothes. "I can't prove it. But I think Jake's the one."

"So what are you going to do?"

"Talk to him about it," Nancy said. "First thing tomorrow morning."

"Hey, Nancy, I wouldn't do that," Daryl said quickly. "Jake Webb's not the kind of guy you go around accusing of something, believe me."

"I believe you," Nancy told him. "I also think he has some explaining to do."

Daryl took her hand, sounding really worried. "You shouldn't mess with that guy, Nancy!"

"I'm not going to mess with him, I'm just going to talk to him." In a way, Nancy was almost glad that Jake had given her something to think about. It took her mind off how she felt about Daryl, which was a mystery she didn't want to solve just then. "Please don't worry. I'll be careful," she said, flagging down a car that was passing slowly. "But Jake Webb is up to something, and I'm going to find out what it is."

"I think Daryl's right," George said as she drove toward Bedford High the next morning. Until Nancy got another car, George and Bess had to play chauffeur. "I think you should steer clear of this Jake Webb and go right to the police. Show them your car. Then let them deal with Jake."

"That's what I think, too." Bess leaned over the back seat and grinned at Nancy. "Now, tell us more about Daryl Gray."

"You'll probably meet him one of these days," Nancy said. She stared out at the beautiful Bedford houses, trying to decide the best way to approach Jake. Daryl was the least of her worries at the moment, even though she couldn't help remembering the kiss he'd given her after driving her home the previous night.

Before he'd kissed her, he'd tried once again to talk her out of confronting Jake. Nancy was touched that he was so worried about her, but she was sure she could handle Jake Webb. After all, she wasn't going to meet him in some dark alley; she was going to walk right up to him in the halls of Bedford High. She couldn't wait to see the look on his face when he saw that his gruesome plan hadn't worked—that she was alive and ready to take him on, the creep!

"What's happening?" George interrupted Nancy's thoughts, pointing to the wide front steps of the high school.

Nancy looked and saw at least half the student body milling around outside. The kids were talking in little clusters, waving their arms, pointing dramatically. Then she saw the police cars, one with its red lights still flashing.

"Well, at least you'll have police protection when you talk to Jake," Bess joked. "I wonder what they're here for?"

"Good question," Nancy said. Could Daryl have called them? She didn't think so. He'd tried to talk her out of dealing with Jake at least ten times, but he'd never once suggested that she go to the police, which was a little strange, when she thought about it.

She didn't think about it for long, though. As soon as she got out of the car, she joined the nearest group of kids.

"What happened?" she asked. "What's going on?"

One of the girls turned to her, fear and excitement in her eyes. "It's Jake Webb," she said breathlessly. "He's been killed!"

Chapter
Seven

NANCY WONDERED FOR a moment if she'd heard right. "Did you say killed—dead?"

"As a doornail!"

"But . . . how?"

"Nobody knows for sure," the girl went on, "but somebody found him about twenty minutes ago, and they say his neck's broken." She shivered. "It's awful, isn't it? I heard the guy who found him is still throwing up. Personally, I'm sure I would have passed out. I mean, can you imagine?"

Nancy could hardly imagine any of it. All night she'd been gearing up, getting ready to face Jake Webb, to accuse him, among other things, of trying to kill her. And in spite of what she'd told Daryl and Bess and George, she *had* been scared. Well, she wouldn't have to be scared anymore, not of Jake Webb.

Still finding the whole thing unbelievable, Nancy reported the news to Bess and George. Then she climbed the front steps and went into school. As she moved through the main hall, she heard bits and pieces of conversation that told her a little more about Jake Webb's demise:

"Right next to the video lab, at the bottom of the stairs—hard, cement stairs. Geez, no wonder the fall broke his neck."

"They say he's been dead for two hours—I wonder what he was doing here at six in the morning?"

"Probably planting a bomb."

"Too bad he fell first."

"Fell? The guy didn't fall, no way! Didn't you hear about his face?"

Jake's face. That's what Nancy heard most about on her walk through the hall. His face was bruised and cut. The bruises could have come from a fall down a flight of cement stairs. But not the cuts around his eyes, not his split lip.

Jake had been in a fight before he hit the hard floor in front of the lab. And if that was true, Nancy thought, then he didn't fall. He was pushed. And if he was pushed, then her investigation had just taken a giant leap—from vandalism to murder.

No one she heard even pretended to feel sorry that Jake was dead, and as she thought about Hunk, Hal, Connie, and who knew how many others, she realized that a lot of people around Bedford High would have wanted Jake to vanish. But who would have wanted it badly enough to give him that push?

When Nancy reached the scene of Jake's "accident," the police and the man from the coroner's office were still gathered there. The body, thank goodness, was gone, but the chalk outline remained.

She knew that if she talked to the police then and there, they'd listen to her. They'd probably even ask her to join their investigation.

But if she did that, she'd blow her cover. And if she did *that,* she might as well kiss the secrets of Bedford High good-bye.

Since the police were busy at the stairwell, Nancy decided that then might be a good time to check Jake Webb's locker. She wanted to look at the contents of that shoebox before anybody else got to it. What besides Connie's bracelet had Jake stashed away?

She was so busy wondering if Jake's locker would have any clues hidden in it, that she didn't see Daryl until she bumped into him.

"Daryl, hi!" Even with everything else on her mind, Nancy felt a warm rush of feeling at the sight of him. "I guess I don't need to ask if you've heard the news?"

"Hardly." Daryl took her hand, but he did it in an absentminded way. "I just talked to Mr. Parton," he said, his voice low enough that only Nancy could hear him. "He told me to tell you it's murder, definitely."

Nancy's eyes widened, but she wasn't really surprised. "Did Mr. Parton say anything about me, about what I should do?"

"Just that he wants you to stay on the case," Daryl whispered, "and to handle it your way."

"Great! I was hoping he'd say that." Nancy breathed a sigh of relief and squeezed Daryl's hand. "Now I can really follow some leads." She started to walk away but Daryl held her back.

"Wait a second," he said. "If Jake was the vandal, then your case is solved. You're into murder now, Nancy. I think you should back off."

"You've got to be kidding!" Nancy couldn't help feeling insulted. "Why should I back off? Do you think it's too complicated for me or something?"

"Hey, no, I didn't mean that." Daryl's violet eyes were full of worry. "It's just that it's probably going to get dangerous, Nancy. You don't have any idea what you're up against."

"No, I don't, but I'm going to find out." Nancy smiled at him. "Thanks for worrying about me, but please try not to," she said. "Really. I can take care of myself." Out of the corner of her eye, she saw Carla Dalton heading toward them, and she couldn't resist planting a kiss on Daryl's cheek. She wanted to anyway, but having Carla as a witness made it even more fun. "Gotta go now," she told Daryl with a twinkle in her eye. "I'll talk to you later, let you know what I've found out."

The halls were still jammed with kids discussing the morning's main event, but luckily the final bell rang as Nancy reached Jake's locker. She was surprised that everyone was still marching to the sound of bells, on that day of all days, but it was a good thing old habits died hard. The hall cleared in a matter of minutes. Nancy pulled on a pair of rubber gloves—no sense leaving fingerprints for the police—and quickly broke into locker 515.

The shoebox was still there, but something else caught her eye first. With a grim smile, she pulled a pair of wire cutters off the shelf. Turning them over in her hands, Nancy thought how easily they must have snapped her brake cable.

Underneath the wire cutters was a small black box. Nancy recognized it immediately as a battery pack for a video camera. She would have bet her fifty-dollar designer jeans that Jake stole it from the video lab and used it to tape her and Bess and George on their shopping spree.

Finally Nancy took out the shoebox and lifted the lid, her heart beating with anticipation. Connie's bracelet was still there, along with a recent article from the school newspaper that carried a picture of Walt Hogan being brutally tackled during a game. The headline read, "The Hunk Gets Hit—He's Down But Not Out." The story went on to explain that if Walt missed the upcoming All-State Championship game because of injury, his badly needed football scholarship—and his ticket to the pros—might be in jeopardy. But Walt pooh-poohed the injury, claiming that nothing would stop him from playing in the All-State game.

At the bottom of the box, folded in half, was a wad of official-looking papers. As Nancy opened them she recognized them at once, without even reading the heading. They were SAT exams. There was just one difference between them and the ones she'd once toiled over—the set of exams in Jake's locker already had the answers marked in.

Nancy studied the curious contents of the box, trying to make sense out of them. She was positive now that Jake was the Bedford High vandal. The battery pack and the SATs pretty much proved that. But, looking at the bracelet, she wondered if he was also into stealing. It didn't really matter if he was, except for one thing—someone had killed him. And Nancy was determined to find out why.

The police were going to be asking the same questions, she knew, so she put the shoebox, the wire cutters, and the battery pack back where she'd found them. She closed the locker door and was trying to come up with an excuse for being late to her first class, when a voice behind her said, "Well, if it isn't Nancy Drew, girl detective. You always manage to be right in the swing of the nastiest things."

Chapter

Eight

NANCY WHIRLED AROUND and came face to face with a tall, black-haired young woman whose vivid red lips were curled in a scornful smile.

Oh, great, Nancy thought. *This is exactly what I need—a snake in the grass like Brenda Carlton!*

As she looked at Brenda, standing there in her trendy trenchcoat, a notebook and pen in one hand, Nancy felt like laughing. Brenda had delusions of being an investigative reporter for *Today's Times,* her daddy's award-winning newspaper. But as far as Nancy was concerned, the only things Brenda did well were wear clothes—and mess up Nancy's investigations. She'd done that too many times for Nancy ever to trust her, and there she was again, smirking and lurking.

"Well, Brenda," Nancy said, "what are you doing here? Trying to play reporter?"

"I saw you first, girl wonder." Brenda gave Nancy a saccharine smile and flipped open her notebook. "Let's see," she said, pretending to scribble with her pen, "'When this reporter arrived at Bedford High, the first person she ran into was none other than Nancy Drew, *alleged* private detective.' How does that sound?"

If she talks any louder, Nancy thought, *the whole school'll know who I am.* "Okay, Brenda, what do you *think* I'm doing here? What do sleuths usually do at the scene of the crime?"

"Scene of the crime? This looks like a high-school locker to me, not the bottom of a stairwell." Brenda's green eyes swept over Nancy in a quick, but all-seeing, glance. Pointing a red-nailed finger at Nancy's history book, she smiled. "Oh, I see! You're posing as a student. How clever of you! I'm surprised you thought of it."

Dropping the sweet voice, Brenda went on, "Now, why don't you give me a few more details about what's going on here? If you don't, all your little high school friends are going to find out real fast what you're really up to. And I have a feeling you wouldn't like that at all."

"Is that a threat, Brenda?"

"Of course it is, Nancy. So how about it? Are you going to give me the whole story?"

Nancy sighed. What choice did she have? The case was complicated and dangerous; she couldn't solve it and battle Brenda Carlton at the same time. "All right," she said, gritting her teeth, "I'll make a deal with you."

"A deal?" Brenda's silky eyebrows drew together in a frown. "What kind of deal?"

"The kind of deal that'll give you the exclusive story," Nancy told her. "Face it, Brenda, the police aren't going to give you the time of day. And right now, I know more about what's going on than they do. So when it's over, I'll be able to give you a really sensational story, right down to the last juicy detail."

Nancy watched Brenda's frown change to a smile. Probably seeing her byline already, she thought. "There's just one catch," she warned. "I give you the story *after* I've solved the case, not before. If you want to know everything I do, stay out of my way and keep your mouth shut about who I am. Think you can manage that?"

For about thirty seconds Brenda wavered between taking her chances with the police then, or making a deal with Nancy for later. Finally she reached a decision. "Well, all right," she said, pouting. "I'll do it your way. But," she warned, "you'd better keep your part of the bargain or the only role you'll ever play again is 'unemployed detective.'"

Nancy bit her lip to keep back any insulting remarks that might blow the deal. But as she watched Brenda stroll away, she promised herself that someday, she was going to close that reporter's notebook for good.

With the police swarming all over the school, Nancy's investigation didn't get very far. All the kids were talking about Jake, of course, but even so, Nancy wasn't able to learn much. All the kids had opinions, but they were just gossip and speculation. Nancy wanted to talk to the three people whom she knew had some connection with Jake—Walt Hogan, Hal Morgan, and Connie Watson. She didn't see Walt at all, and Hal didn't hear her call to him after American history, or maybe he didn't want to hear her. He looked extremely nervous. So did Connie, who once more acted as if Nancy had developed a sudden case of overwhelmingly bad breath.

If anyone has any answers, Nancy thought, *they're not admitting it.* Nancy didn't have any answers either, but she thought she might find something in the video lab. Obviously, Jake had been "borrowing" the school's video equipment; maybe Nancy could find some clue in the lab that would tell her why.

The door was locked again, so Nancy used her credit card. As she worked the lock, she thought she heard a noise coming from inside the lab. She stopped, listening. There it was, a faint thump, as if someone had dropped something on the floor.

Could a policeman be in there? It was four o'clock in the afternoon; the halls were empty of students, and Nancy had watched the two patrol cars drive off half an hour ago. Still, they might have left one officer behind to guard the school. If they had, Nancy decided that it wouldn't help her case any to get caught.

She raised her hand and knocked loudly on the door. Then she listened again. No sound this time. After a few more loud raps, she decided that whatever she'd heard hadn't come from inside. The empty halls picked up sounds from everywhere. The noise could have come from the floor above. She worked the lock again and pushed open the door.

The room was a wreck. Cables and wires were strewn across the floor like uncoiled snakes, and at least half the tapes had been pulled from the shelves and lay in scattered piles on the desk and the floor. Nancy knew the police must have searched the place after finding that battery pack in Jake's locker. Either that (and they were real slobs), or somebody else had been there. Could that someone have been Jake's murderer, after some kind of evidence?

Suddenly Nancy didn't like all the silence around her. She cleared her throat noisily and told herself that if the murderer had been there, he (or she) was probably long gone. And from the look of things, he hadn't found what he was after. Maybe she could beat him to it, she thought.

Quietly Nancy closed the door behind her and stepped over several lengths of cable to the middle of the room. Her gaze fell on a neat row of about thirty tapes, still on the shelf.

Nancy crossed the room to the shelf and saw that the tapes were just rock videos. Glancing at the familiar names, Nancy thought maybe they weren't worth her attention. But then, one of the labels caught her eye. Right next to "Material Girl" (which made her think immediately of Brenda Carlton) was a tape labeled "I Spy."

"I Spy"? It wasn't any rock group Nancy had heard of. Maybe I Spy was a Bedford High group. Nancy decided to have a quick look at it. She just hoped the music was good.

After the first few seconds Nancy wished there *were* music. The tape was completely silent, but the images were so unbelievable that music would have made it seem like a joke, or some kind of fantasy. Instead, Nancy knew she was seeing reality.

The first person on the tape was Hunk Hogan. He was sitting on a bench in what must have been the locker room. No one else was visible, and when Walt glanced cautiously around, Nancy decided that *he* had decided he was alone.

After another careful look, the star tackle reached into the duffel bag at his feet and took out a roll of white tape. Obviously in great pain, he began to wrap it around his rib cage, wincing the whole time. Nancy remembered the article in Jake's locker that told of Walt betting all his hopes for a football scholarship on the upcoming All-State game. From the look of him, he'd be lucky to get dressed for that game, much less play in it. Walt was hurt, but he'd hidden it—from everyone except Jake Webb.

The video lab was stuffy and hot, but Nancy shivered as a chill ran up her spine. She'd been right—this case was much, much bigger than anyone thought. And the "I Spy" tape was an extremely hot piece of evidence. Too hot to be watching smack in the middle of Bedford High.

Quickly Nancy pushed the stop button and ejected the tape. She was reaching for the monitor to shut it off when she heard a noise. Or thought she did. She snapped off the monitor and listened. For a few seconds the only sound she heard was the blood pulsing in her ears. But then came another noise, a squeak, as if someone had stopped leaning on a table. Or a door!

At the far end of the room was a door marked "Supplies," and as Nancy listened again, she heard another muffled sound. Someone was in that supply room. And it wasn't a policeman. A policeman would have been out by then, asking her what she was doing there, demanding that she turn over the tape, which was crucial evidence in a murder investigation. And who else would be interested in such crucial evidence but Jake's killer?

For an instant Nancy froze. If the killer was in that supply closet, Nancy's life was in danger. So was the evidence. She knew she had to get out fast. Noiselessly she dropped the videotape into her bag. She wanted to run, but she was afraid of alerting whoever was behind the door. Slowly, quietly, she inched her way across the lab to the hall door. With a sweaty hand, she eased it open and slipped out. Then she tore down the hall as fast as she could.

It was late afternoon and the hall was dark. The stairs leading to the first floor were even darker, but Nancy didn't slow down. She jumped the last four steps, skidded around a corner, and raced toward the main door. As she neared it she thought she heard footsteps on the stairs, but she didn't bother to turn around and make sure. Still moving fast, she rammed into the panic bar, expecting the door to fly open.

The door didn't budge! Nancy was certain she heard footsteps behind her. She gave the door another desperate push. Nothing.

Okay, she thought. I guess it's showdown time. Taking a deep breath, Nancy turned around, ready to face the intruder.

Chapter

Nine

Nancy closed her eyes, waited a beat, then forced them open. The dark hall loomed ahead of her. She focused on the bottom of the staircase, held her breath, and waited again. All she saw were shadows, and all she heard was her own heartbeat. No one was there. Not now, anyway.

Letting out her breath in a sigh of relief, Nancy leaned against the door—and found herself falling backward as the door opened easily, depositing her on her rear on the stone steps outside.

Of course, she thought, picking herself up,

it's a double door. You just pushed the wrong side.

Glad to be outdoors, Nancy took several deep gulps of the cool autumn air. Then she saw George's car make a slow turn around the side of the building.

"Hey!" Nancy waved her hand and ran down the front steps. "Here I am!"

The car slowed, and Bess stuck her head out the window. "We were just about to give up and go home," she said. "George has been driving around this parking lot forever, but I kept telling her you probably got a ride with Daryl."

"I wish I *had* been with Daryl," Nancy said as she climbed into the back seat. "He's a lot more fun. And a lot safer, too."

"Why? What happened?" George wanted to know.

As they drove away from Bedford High, Nancy filled them in on everything that had happened, from the details of Jake's murder to her own scary escape from the video lab. "And wait'll you see the tape," she said, patting her duffel bag. "It'll never win an Oscar, but it's one of the most fascinating movies I've ever seen."

When they got back to Nancy's River Heights home and settled down to watch, they soon discovered that the tape was even more fascinating than Nancy had predicted. And Walt

Hogan wasn't the only person Jake had made into a star.

Bess sighed as she watched Hunk tape his ribs. "How can he stand to play when he's in pain?"

"It's his only chance for that scholarship," George said. "If he doesn't get that, he'll never make the pros."

"Yeah, and he wasn't about to let anything stand in his way," Nancy commented. "Not the pain, and not Jake."

"Poor guy." Bess sighed again. "At least Jake Webb can't bother him anymore. Do you suppose Hunk is glad, deep down, that Jake's dead?"

"He wouldn't be human if he weren't," Nancy said. "But I have a question for you. Do you suppose Walt Hogan had anything to do with getting rid of Jake?"

Before either of her friends had a chance to answer that startling question, another face appeared on the television screen—the smooth, round face of Connie Watson.

"Who's that?" Bess asked.

"A girl from Bedford High," Nancy told her, and scooted to the edge of the couch, wondering what on earth shy Connie could possibly have done to get a part in Jake Webb's "movie."

She soon found out. The "setting" was a

sidewalk sale in fashionably quaint downtown Bedford. All the shopowners had brought their wares out to the sidewalks on what looked like a sunny autumn day. Crowds of shoppers strolled by, eating ice cream cones and stopping to look at paintings, handmade pottery, and furniture, and, Nancy noticed with a sense of dread, jewelry.

Nancy knew what was coming the minute she saw the jewelry display. Sure enough, the camera panned the crowd and focused on Connie Watson, a large shopping bag in her hand.

Nancy's heart sank as she watched what happened next. Connie picked up a bracelet— the one Nancy had seen her wearing—and admired it for a minute. Then she seemed to ask the shopowner the price and reluctantly put it back on the display table.

"Now just watch," Nancy told her friends. "She's about to make the biggest mistake of her life."

Hovering at the edge of the jewelry table, Connie waited until the owner was busy with about six customers at once. Then a close-up, courtesy of Jake the cameraman, showed her hook a finger under the bracelet and slide it into her conveniently waiting shopping bag. The camera pulled back then, and Connie melted into the crowds that filled the sidewalk.

But Jake wasn't through with Connie. His

next shot caught her going up the front steps of the high school, the early morning sun glinting on her new gold bracelet.

"So far we've seen somebody covering up an injury and somebody shoplifting," George said. "I wonder what's next?"

"I'm not sure I want to know," Bess shuddered. "This whole thing gives me the creeps."

"Oh, no!" Nancy pointed to the television screen and shook her head in amazement. "It's Hal Morgan. I should have guessed."

The next installment of Jake's horror show followed Hal, nervous nail-chewer and future Harvard scholar, straight to the door of the office of Bedford High's principal. Like Walt Hogan, Hal probably thought he was alone, because he glanced furtively around before entering the office.

The camera didn't follow him inside. It held steady on the closed door. Five seconds passed and then the door opened. Out came Hal, who stood still, obviously trying to work something out in his mind.

"You can almost hear the wheels turning," George remarked. "He's empty-handed. I wonder what he's after."

"Answers," Nancy said.

Bess looked confused. "Huh?"

"Just keep watching," Nancy told her. "You'll see what I mean."

Having worked out the problem, Hal walked

quickly to another door. Without bothering to look behind him, he opened it and went inside. The camera stayed on the sign on the door, which read, "Counselors' Offices."

When Hal came out this time, he wasn't empty-handed. He didn't look worried or confused anymore, either. The camera gave Nancy and her two friends a brief glimpse of Hal's triumphant smile, but it lingered longest on what he held in his hands—answer books for the Scholastic Aptitude Tests.

"How could Jake tape that without Hal seeing him?" George asked.

"He really knew his video stuff," Nancy said. "He probably set that one up by remote control. That would explain why the offices had been broken into earlier. He must have been rigging up the camera." She thought a minute. "I wouldn't even be surprised if he gave Hal the idea for stealing those answers, just so he could tape the whole thing. After all, Jake did work in the principal's office."

Wavering black bars and dancing snowflakes had appeared on the screen, and Nancy turned off the VCR and the television. "I'm glad that's over," she commented.

"So am I." Bess stood up and stretched. "I don't know why, but movies always make me hungry, even this one. Let's go see what's in the refrigerator."

In the refrigerator they found leftover takeout Chinese food. Sitting at the round oak kitchen table, the three friends discussed Jake's tape between bites of lo mein and shrimp fried rice.

"Obviously, Connie didn't buy that bracelet," Nancy said. "She stole it. And after Hal lost so much ground trying to become class president, he knew the only way he'd get into Harvard was to cheat on the SAT so that he could get unusually high scores."

Bess poured herself some more diet soda. "And poor Hunk. It must be awful to feel so desperate!"

"Why do you think Jake did it?" George asked. "Money?"

"Maybe." Nancy crunched thoughtfully on an ice cube. "But I think it was more of a power trip. He would find someone's weak spot and dig in. Jake liked knowing everybody's secrets. That's probably how he found out about me in time to tape us at the mall that day. He must have had his ear to Mr. Parton's door when Mr. Parton talked to my father. He knew my 'secret,' too. He liked being king of the mountain."

"Yeah, well somebody finally pushed him off," Bess said. "And no wonder. He must have had things on half the kids in school."

"But he only has three people on tape," George pointed out. "Nancy, do you really think one of them killed him?"

Nancy shrugged her shoulders in frustration.

Later, after George and Bess had left, she took a long hot shower, trying to come up with an answer to George's question.

Walt Hogan was strong enough to give Jake that final push, she thought, especially if he'd been angry. And Hal wasn't exactly a lightweight. If he'd been desperate enough, he might just have decided to challenge Jake.

She couldn't rule out Connie either. Sweet, gossipy Connie Watson was as strong a candidate for murderer as the two guys. Anyone could have pushed him.

Nancy turned around and let the warm, misty spray roll off her back. Jake Webb wasn't just a thief and a vandal, she thought, he was the Bedford High Blackmailer. Getting power from kids who'd made mistakes must have given him a kick, a sick, sadistic kick.

But somebody had finally kicked him back. The question was, who? Was it really one of the kids on the tape—Walt or Connie or Hal? Could one of those three Bedford High students have been so determined to get out from under Jake's thumb that he or she murdered him to keep a secret safe?

Chapter
Ten

NANCY PUSHED HER sloppy joe aside and reached for Daryl's hand across the cafeteria table. "I need a favor."

"Just ask," Daryl said with a smile. "What? You need a ride home after school?"

"Not exactly," Nancy answered, looking mysterious. "I lucked out. This morning my dad surprised me with a new Mustang GT Convertible."

Daryl rolled his eyes. "You've got to be kidding."

"The deal is I'll pay him back when the insurance money comes through." Nancy grinned sheepishly. "Plus twenty years allowance, I've been told."

"Poor baby," Daryl teased her, leaning close enough to brush his lips against her ear. "So what's the favor? You want me to test-drive your new toy?"

Nancy didn't tease back. "No," she said, forcing herself to pull back from Daryl's handsome face. "I want to tell you something, but you have to promise not to breathe a word of it to anyone."

"I can keep a secret, Detective. Promise."

They were alone at a table in the farthest corner of the cafeteria. Any of the kids who happened to glance their way probably thought they were having a private lovers' talk. But love was the farthest thing from Nancy's mind at that moment as she quietly told Daryl about Jake Webb's blackmail videotape.

When she finished, she sat back and sipped her iced tea, waiting for Daryl's reaction.

But Daryl must have been so stunned he couldn't think of anything to say. He just stared at her with wide, dark-blue eyes, his face almost blank.

"It's okay to be shocked," Nancy said. "I was, and I'm the detective."

"Yeah, I . . ." Daryl shook his head and whistled softly. "Wow. I *am* shocked. I mean, it's unbelievable."

"It is—unless you've seen the tape."

"So what are you going to do with it?" Daryl asked. "Turn it over to the police?"

Nancy shook her head. "I guess I'll have to give it to them pretty soon. But since Mr. Parton is letting me handle this my way, I'd like to work on my own just a little longer. For now, that tape's going to stay safe at home, where I can keep an eye on it."

Daryl nodded. "I guess you think one of those kids killed Jake, huh?"

"I don't know what I think yet," Nancy admitted. "I don't want to believe it at all."

"But they're the only ones on the tape, isn't that what you said?" Daryl asked quickly.

"Yes, but somehow I just . . ." Nancy sighed.

"Jake really blew it for everybody, didn't he?" Daryl looked sympathetic and concerned, just the way Ned would have reacted, Nancy thought. Then Daryl leaned across the table and gave her one of his sexiest looks. "Don't take this wrong, Detective, but be careful, okay?"

Warmed by Daryl's concern and support, not to mention his touch, Nancy spent the rest of the afternoon—in between classes—tracking down the three "stars" of Jake's videotape.

She found Hal in the library, just beginning a

paper that she happened to know was due in two days. "Hi," she whispered as she joined him at the study table. "I thought you'd be finished with that by now. Everybody says you're a real whiz."

Hal gave her a nervous smile and shrugged. "Even whizzes get behind sometimes."

"Well, I guess you don't have to worry, though," Nancy went on. "I mean, if you're smart enough to get into Harvard and write papers for Jake Webb on the side, then—"

That got Hal's attention. "What do you mean?" he interrupted in a whisper. "I don't know what you're talking about."

"Really?" Nancy was all innocence. "Gee, I was sure I heard you and Jake talking about it in the hall, right after that pop quiz, remember?"

"No. You didn't. I mean, you must have heard wrong." Hal stood up, gathering his stuff together with shaky hands. "Look, I've got to get going."

"Oh, too bad," Nancy said. "I was going to ask your advice. See, I'll be taking the SATs soon and I thought maybe you could give me some hints on how to handle them. Everybody says your scores were sky-high. How did you do it? Or is that a secret?"

Hal looked so nervous, Nancy thought he might break down right there in the library. But he managed to hold himself together long enough to mumble something about "luck." Then he rushed out of the room, but not before shooting Nancy a look of pure terror.

Nancy wasn't sure what to make of it. Was Hal scared because of the SATs he'd stolen, or had he done something much worse than stealing and cheating? She decided to try again with him, but first she wanted to talk to the other two.

Walt Hogan wasn't hard to find. He stood out like a redwood in a grove of saplings, and she spotted him right before fifth period, heading out one of the side doors. *Good,* she said to herself. *You were looking for an excuse to cut calculus anyway.*

Nancy followed Walt across the campus toward the track, where she watched him run two laps before he stopped, throwing himself down on the grass. He was gasping as if he'd just run a three-minute mile, and she figured he must still be in pain.

"Tired?" Nancy asked pleasantly as she dropped into the grass beside him.

"Yeah." Walt grunted a couple of times and then opened his eyes. "Do I know you?"

"Well, we met," Nancy said. "Monday, remember? We sort of bumped into each other in the hall and Daryl Gray introduced us. I'm Nancy Drew."

"Yeah, sure." Walt didn't look sure at all. "How's it going?"

"Fine." Nancy plucked some grass and twisted it around her finger. "I watched you at practice the other day," she said. "You really amaze me. I mean, I fell off the trampoline and I could barely walk, so I know what you're going through."

"What do you mean, what I'm going through?" Walt asked.

"The pain," Nancy said. "Jake Webb told me all about—"

"Webb?" Walt broke in. "What kind of business did you have with that scum?"

"No business," Nancy said quickly. "He just explained about your injury and I wanted you to know that I understand."

"Look!" Walt jumped to his feet and stood towering over her. "I don't know what that slime told you, but whatever it was, he was lying!"

Nancy got to her feet and faced him. "Hey, okay," she said. "Don't get excited. I just thought—"

"Don't think!" Walt shouted. He took a step toward Nancy, and for a second she thought he was going to hit her. "Just get out of my sight! There's no pain because there's no injury, you understand?"

With an angry glare, Walt turned and slowly

walked toward the school. Nancy let her breath out. She'd taken a few judo classes, but not nearly enough to prepare her to face a raging, 200-pound football player.

Walt was touchy, to put it mildly, but Nancy still didn't have anything more than suspicions to go on. *No more hinting,* she told herself. *With Connie, just come right out and say what's on your mind. As horrible as the truth is, you have to confront her with it. At least you won't have to worry about being attacked. You hope.*

Chapter

Eleven

NANCY FOUND CONNIE Watson in the gym after school, watching cheerleader practice. She climbed the bleachers to her side.

"I have to talk to you," she said quietly. "About Jake Webb. And your bracelet. And a videotape I found."

Connie's round face flushed and then drained of color until it resembled a full moon. "I . . . I don't . . ." she stammered.

"Look," Nancy went on, ignoring the girl's panicked eyes, "the police found your bracelet in Jake's locker. And I know it's yours because I saw the videotape—the one Jake made of you stealing it. I haven't shown it to the police yet. But I will unless you tell me everything you know about how Jake was murdered."

Tears ran down Connie's cheeks, making them glisten under the bright gym lights. "It all started at the beginning of the school year. See, that bracelet wasn't the only thing I stole," she admitted. "I took a sweater the first time, and it was so easy I decided to try for a jacket." Connie swallowed hard. "Only that time I got caught. It's all in my school file."

"And since Jake worked in the office, he found out about it," Nancy commented.

Connie nodded and took a shaky breath. "I didn't know he knew, of course. But then, after I took the bracelet . . . Well, I know it was wrong but I wanted it so much, and there was no way I could afford it! I promised myself it was the last time. But then . . ."

She wiped her face and sniffed loudly. ". . . Then Jake came strutting along, said he had a 'movie' he wanted me to see. I nearly died when I saw it! I told him I was going to return the bracelet, but that slug made me wear it. When I tried to get rid of it, he stopped me and kept it himself. He said he knew all about my shoplifting record and that if he told anyone about the bracelet, I'd probably go to jail. And he was right!

"So after that, I had to do everything he asked." Connie shuddered. "Everything. I hoped that when he died, my secret would die with him."

Nancy felt terrible, but she had to keep pushing or she'd never get to the bottom of the mystery. "But Jake didn't just die," she said. "Someone killed him."

"I know, I know," Connie moaned. Then she looked at Nancy sharply. "I didn't do it! I'm not sorry he's dead, but I didn't kill him—and I can't believe you think I might have!"

With a sob, Connie ran down the bleacher steps and out of the gym. Nancy felt helpless. She wished she could have told Connie everything would be okay. But Connie had as much reason to knock off Jake as anyone else he'd blackmailed. Until Nancy found out who did it, she couldn't afford to feel sorry for anybody, not even sweet Connie Watson.

Still thinking about the answers she didn't have, Nancy left the gym and walked outside to her car. Daryl Gray was leaning against the driver's door, and Nancy's stomach did a little flip at the sight of him.

"I can tell by the look on your face that your 'interviews' didn't go too well," he said when she reached his side.

"You're right," Nancy admitted. "I'm not much further along than I was last night. But I'll figure it out eventually." She looked at him with a mock frown. "What are you doing here, anyway? I didn't think you'd ever come within fifty feet of a car of mine."

"When you want to be with somebody enough, you have to take chances." Daryl put a hand on Nancy's shoulder and brought his lips close to her ear. "Besides," he whispered, "I have an ulterior motive." He pulled open the door for her. "What I really want, aside from spending some time with you, is to see that tape."

"You mean 'The Secrets of Bedford High?'"

"Yeah. It sounds wild." Daryl shut the door after her and leaned down, his head in the window. "No, really, I thought maybe I could help. I know all those people better than you do. Maybe I can find some clues."

"It sounds good to me," Nancy said. "Let's go."

"You lead, I'll follow," Daryl said, and walked off toward his Porsche.

Half an hour later, the two of them were in Nancy's house, sitting close together on the beige couch in the den, sipping Cokes and looking at the Jake Webb production.

Daryl watched carefully but didn't say much, and Nancy was acutely aware of his closeness in the darkened room. As Connie Watson faded into the crowds of shoppers, Daryl brought his arm up and around Nancy's shoulder, his hand resting lightly on the back of her neck.

By the time Connie was walking up the

school steps, neither Daryl nor Nancy was watching. Their eyes were on each other.

"I hate to tell you this," Daryl said softly, "but I didn't see anything that might help you out."

"That's okay," Nancy whispered. "I'm glad you came over anyway."

As if they'd both thought of it at the same time, they moved their heads closer together until their lips were touching. Nancy slid her hands up Daryl's arms, felt his thick blond hair under her fingers, felt his lips press against hers. She could hear her heart pounding in her ears, and then suddenly she heard another sound— the doorbell.

Reluctant, but almost relieved, Nancy disentangled herself from Daryl's arms and stood up. "Bad timing, huh?"

"The worst," Daryl groaned ruefully.

The doorbell chimed again and Nancy went down the hall to answer it.

"Nan, hi!" Bess's smile changed to a gape as she stared at Nancy. "Were you taking a nap or something?"

"No, why?"

"You look a little . . . wrinkled," George pointed out.

"No, I was just—" Nancy stopped when she realized that her friends were staring at something behind her. Turning, she saw Daryl walking down the hall toward them, smoothing his hair with one hand and straightening his shirt with the other.

After a quick introduction Daryl turned to Nancy. "I think I'd better get going," he said with a warm smile. "See you tomorrow, okay?"

Bess could hardly wait until he was out the door. "Wow," she said breathily. "No wonder you look so glassy-eyed, Nancy. He's gorgeous!"

"For once I can't argue," George said.

"If I hadn't just met somebody else," Bess went on, "—and by the way, his name's Alan Wales, Nancy, wait'll you see him—I'd definitely fall in love with Daryl Gray. What were you two up to, anyway?"

Nancy was saved from explaining by another bell—the telephone. "Nancy," Hannah called from the kitchen. "It's for you. It's Ned."

"Thanks, Hannah," Nancy called back. "I'll take it in my bedroom." With a flustered smile, she turned to Bess and George. "I'll meet you in the den in a couple of minutes. Oh, turn off the tape machine, would you? I forgot."

"I can't imagine why," Bess teased.

Alone in her room Nancy tried to compose herself before she picked up the extension. Would Ned hear anything in her voice that would reveal what she'd just done? She hoped not. After all, Daryl was exciting, but Ned Nickerson was the one she loved. Wasn't he?

"Ned?"

"Hey, Nancy. How're you doing? I miss you."

She could hear the smile in his voice. "I miss you, too," she told him. "How's life at the university?"

"Busy. I've got good news, but first, tell me how the case is going."

"Well, I'll put it this way—it's still going." Nancy didn't really want to get into it. She might have to mention Daryl and she wasn't ready for that. "What's your good news?"

"I'm coming down this weekend."

"To River Heights?"

"Where else? That's where *you* are, isn't it?" Ned laughed. "What's the matter, don't you want to see me?"

"Are you kidding? Of course I do!" Nancy could say that truthfully, but still, she wondered what the weekend would be like. After all, she had a date with Daryl for the dance. What would Ned think about that? "When will you get here?" she asked.

"Tomorrow, early afternoon sometime. I'll call you as soon as I get there. Nancy?" Ned lowered his voice. "I can't wait to see you. Let's do something special."

"You're on," Nancy said with a grin, although she couldn't imagine what they'd do, not if she was busy with Daryl.

After she hung up, she tried to figure out whether to tell Ned everything about the case, including her two "close encounters" with Daryl, or to keep those incidents a secret and just pass Daryl off as one of her contacts in the case.

She was staring at the phone and chewing on a fingernail when George stuck her head around the door. "Nancy? Could you come in the den? There's something you should see."

Glad to be distracted, Nancy followed George down the hall and into the den. "Bess was just about to turn the VCR off when something came on," George explained. "I guess Jake had one more scene and he put it at the very end of the tape."

"Who is it?" Nancy asked. "What other poor slob did Jake have in the wringer?"

"Oh, Nancy, it's not just another poor slob," Bess said. "Look."

George pushed the play button and a face appeared on the television screen. Nancy didn't say a word. She couldn't. The face belonged to Daryl Gray!

Chapter

Twelve

IN DISBELIEVING SILENCE Nancy watched her
"contact" in front of an unseen video camera.
She had to keep reminding herself that it wasn't
a performance. It was for real.

Scene One—Daryl got into his Porsche and
drove off, the camera lingering on a sign for
Route 110 East.

Scene Two—The Porsche pulled into the
parking lot of a tacky-looking diner called the
Red Caboose. Daryl got out of the car, walked
across the street, and stood waiting on the
sidewalk. Jake had obviously stayed behind,
hidden somewhere in the Red Caboose lot.

Scene Three—A heavyset man with thick hair and a bushy mustache joined Daryl on the sidewalk. Jake zoomed in for a closer shot. The camera zeroed in on an identification tag clipped to the man's pocket. Nancy tried desperately to read the name. She thought she could make out an *M* and a *D,* but she wasn't sure. Jake hadn't been able to get a tight enough shot. Daryl and the man exchanged a few words, and then the man handed Daryl a small envelope, which Daryl stuffed in his jeans pocket. The man walked away, revealing on the chain-link fence behind him a sign, about one foot square. The letters were unreadable.

Scene Four—Another shot of Daryl in his car, this time passing the high school on Bedford Road.

Scene Five—The Porsche turned into a drive. No house was visible from the road, just an intricately scrolled wrought-iron fence on each side of the drive.

That was it. Five short scenes that blew Nancy's world apart. Less than an hour earlier, she'd been in Daryl's arms, a victim of his warm eyes and smooth personality. Then suddenly she'd discovered that he, too, was a victim of Jake Webb's scheming mind.

A few things began to make sense—the way Daryl had tried to talk her out of dealing with Jake, his eagerness to know how the case was going and to see the tape. With a shudder,

Nancy wondered what would have happened if he'd stayed long enough to see himself on the screen. Would he have killed Nancy for the tape, the way he might—just might—have killed Jake?

Pushing that awful thought from her mind, Nancy jumped up and turned the tape off. Then she started pacing around the room.

"Nancy," Bess asked, "are you okay?"

"Just totally confused." Nancy managed a laugh. "I mean, obviously Jake had something on Daryl. But what? The tape really doesn't show him doing anything wrong."

"It doesn't show much of anything," Bess agreed. "He just went someplace, met a man, and then went someplace else. I know!" she said. "Maybe he had a gambling thing going. You know, running numbers."

That made sense, Nancy thought. After all, with his father practically bankrupt, Daryl would want to keep up his slick lifestyle somehow. Gambling wasn't so terrible, she told herself hopefully.

"Well, we're not getting anywhere sitting around talking about it," George pointed out.

"You're right. Let's get going. I want to try to follow Daryl's route on the tape." Nancy grabbed the keys to her car. "We know what the others did. Now let's find out what Daryl's secret is."

Nancy's new car sped along Route 110. "Just

keep your eyes open for that diner," she reminded her friends.

"I won't miss it," Bess said. "I'm famished."

"We're not going there to eat," George told her.

"I know, but it wouldn't hurt to get a takeout order. I was so busy with Alan that I didn't even get lunch. Oh, Nancy," Bess went on, "I can't wait for you to meet Alan! He's not only good-looking, he's talented."

"At what?"

"He plays the guitar, and he's really serious about it. I'm sure he'll be a superstar someday," Bess said loyally. "Oh, I just remembered! His group's playing for the Bedford High dance tomorrow night!"

"Hey!" cried George. "Look on your right! It's the Red Caboose."

Just as Daryl had done, Nancy pulled into the parking lot, and the three girls got out. Facing away from the diner, across Route 110, they could see the chain-link fence, and now that they had a full view, they could see several of the small, square signs attached to the fence at regular intervals.

Beyond the fence was a vast complex of buildings. As Nancy and her friends crossed the street to the sidewalk where Daryl had met the man, Nancy wondered if the buildings were a factory of some kind.

Bess reached the fence first. " 'Private—

Authorized Personnel Only,'" she read from one of the signs. Then she was quiet as Nancy and George joined her and read what was printed below that, in smaller letters. "U.S. Government."

"I didn't know there were any government offices out here," George said. "What is it, I wonder. A research place or something?"

"Let's find out," Nancy said. "I'm sure anybody who works at the Red Caboose knows what it is." She spoke calmly, but inside she was becoming very nervous. What could Daryl possibly have to do with the U.S. Government?

"It's an Air Force defense plant, honey," the man behind the counter said, in answer to Nancy's question. "They're up to their ears in secrets over there—designs for bombs, blueprints for nifty little radar devices that'll track down a missile before it's even left the ground, stuff like that." He gave the counter a swipe with his dishcloth and shook his head. "Tell you the truth, I get scared sometimes. If the United States is ever attacked, you can bet some country's got a bomb picked out for that place. And you know what that means for the Red Caboose."

Nancy and George were reeling from the idea that Daryl might be involved in spying somehow. Bess tried to perk them up as they walked out to the car. "Look," she said hopefully, "it might not be as bad as it seems. We don't know what that man on the tape gave Daryl. Maybe Daryl started a private messenger service."

"Maybe," Nancy said. But her thoughts were whirling around madly. Jake wouldn't have bothered with Daryl if Daryl were innocent. But what exactly was he guilty of? And how big was this case going to get? It had started out as petty vandalism, then it moved up to blackmail, and then to murder. Now what? Could it really be espionage? "Let's take a ride to Bedford," she said. "I want to find out exactly where Daryl delivered that envelope. That must be what he did, even though Jake didn't get it on tape."

It was dark by the time they reached Bedford Road, and as they drove by the high school, the road became darker. This was the super-rich section of Bedford, "The Mansion Mile," as Nancy had heard someone in school call it. But from the road, with high shrubbery and thick groves of trees masking the grounds, it was hard to see any landmarks.

Finally, though, George spotted the wrought-iron fence they'd seen on the tape, and Nancy turned into what seemed like a private drive. There was no gate and no sign to tell them whose property they were on.

"What do we do now?" Bess asked. "Pretend we're lost?"

"Good idea." Nancy drove through the opening in the fence.

As soon as they were on the property, the drive curved sharply to reveal a gate anchored to two moss-covered pillars. In the glare of the headlights the girls could easily read the sign posted on the gate: "U.S.S.R.—Private Property."

"U.S.S.R.?" Bess said. "What country are we in, anyway?"

"I think it's an estate, a kind of compound for diplomats," George told them. "I remember reading that a lot of countries buy foreign property so their officials can have someplace to go to relax. We're not all that far from the U.N., you know."

"We're not all that far from the defense plant, either," Nancy said.

Before anyone had a chance to comment on that remark, the gate swung open and searchlights flooded the area. The girls heard the sound of an engine and saw a pair of headlights round a curve in the drive in front of them. The headlights were getting closer fast, and they were heading straight for Nancy's car!

Chapter

Thirteen

THE FLOODLIGHTS LIT up the Mustang, throwing everything outside it into pitch darkness, except for the two headlights. They were dancing over the bumpy drive, looming closer and closer.

"Who do you suppose that is?" Bess squinted in the glare. "It's coming awfully fast!"

George cleared her throat. "Somehow, I don't think it's a welcoming committee."

"Let's get out of here!" cried Nancy.

As the headlights approached the gate, Nancy stepped on the gas, steered the Mustang into a tire-screeching U-turn, and peeled out of the drive. Just as they neared Bedford Road,

Bess let out a faint shriek and pointed to a clump of bushes at the end of the drive.

Nancy gasped. Jumping over the bushes and onto the drive directly in front of her car were two figures. In the beam of the headlights, the girls could see that they were men, dressed in black jumpsuits of some kind. One was hefting a long-barreled pistol. The other was unslinging a rifle from his shoulder.

Instinctively Nancy moved her foot onto the brake pedal. But then she stopped. "What am I doing?" she said. "If they think I'm going to slow down and make small talk while a gun is pointed at me, they're crazy!"

Nancy moved her foot back to the gas pedal and stepped on it, mashing down on the horn at the same time. Bess put her hands over her eyes, but George and Nancy saw the two men hold their pose—legs wide apart, guns at the ready—for about two seconds. Then, as the Mustang bore down on them, they jumped aside. Wheels spinning and gravel flying, the car swerved sharply onto Bedford Road.

"Are we going to live?" Bess asked.

"Not if we don't hurry," Nancy answered. "Look."

Behind them, turning out of the private drive and coming fast, was a dark-colored, unmarked van.

"It's not over yet," Nancy said. "Let's see how far they're willing to go."

Except for Nancy's car and the van, Bedford Road was nearly deserted. Nancy raced the car past other estates, past the high school, past a solitary jogger in white. The van stayed close behind, not losing an inch.

Suddenly Nancy saw a traffic light ahead of her. It was green, and Nancy eased up on the gas pedal.

"What are you doing?" Bess cried. "They'll catch us!"

"Maybe, maybe not." Nancy slowed as much as possible, keeping her eyes on the traffic light. Behind them, the van's headlights were bright enough to read by. The light changed to amber and Nancy felt a jolt as the van rammed into the back of her car.

George's head snapped back as the van once again made contact with the Mustang. "Uh, Nancy," she said, "if you're going to do what I think you're going to do, do it now. The light's been yellow for five seconds."

"Right. Hang on!" Nancy pushed the gas pedal and raced through the intersection just after the light turned red. The van's brakes screeched, but then its driver decided to risk running a light. It tore through the intersection only a few feet behind the Mustang.

Nancy shook her head in disbelief. "Where are the police when you really need them?" she joked. Actually, she was glad that a police car hadn't been lurking at the intersection. A high-speed chase through the streets of Bedford might get the driver of the van in trouble. But when he showed his diplomatic papers or whatever he carried around with him, he'd be off the hook. Then Nancy could do one of two things—blow her cover or get arrested. Neither choice was very appealing.

Reluctantly Nancy slowed the car to a respectable speed. "Anybody got any suggestions?" she asked.

Bess spoke up immediately. "Let's eat."

"Oh, Bess," George said with a moan. "Get serious, will you? There's a lunatic on our tail."

"I *am* serious," Bess protested. "There's a pizza place just ahead on the right, and it looks jammed. Do you really think those creeps would follow us in there?"

"I'm ready to try anything," Nancy said, and swerved sharply into the parking lot of Guido's Pizza. As she squeezed the car into the last available space, she glanced into the rearview mirror. The van slowed for a moment, then sped down the block and out of sight.

"It worked," she said, with a shaky laugh. "You were right, Bess. I guess it would have blown their image if they'd followed us to Guido's and shot us over a pepperoni pie."

"Speaking of pepperoni," Bess said, "I really am starving."

"So am I," Nancy agreed. "Let's go pig out."

Guido's was jammed, as Bess had predicted,

but the three girls managed to find a table near the kitchen door. As Nancy sank into a chair, she glanced around and saw several kids from Bedford High, including Carla Dalton. *Terrific,* she thought, *Carla's a quick way to ruin an appetite.* Carla was talking to somebody whose back was to Nancy. She was so involved in whatever she was saying that she didn't notice anyone else.

When their pizza arrived, Nancy discovered that not even Carla Dalton could kill her appetite. Hungrily, she and Bess and George wolfed down slices of the big pie, not saying much of anything. When only one slice was left, Nancy leaned back in her chair and sipped her Coke. "Well, we finally know what Daryl's secret is," she said quietly, "and it's a lot worse than shoplifting."

Bess nodded. "It's really unbelievable, though. I mean, a high-school kid involved in spying? Who would ever guess?"

"That was probably the point," George said. "But Daryl's not the worst one. That man from the defense plant and probably one of the diplomats—they're the real bad guys."

"Daryl's not squeaky clean, though," Nancy remarked. "I'm sure he knew exactly what he was doing." She wasn't really shocked anymore, just angry. And she was more angry at herself than at Daryl. If only she hadn't been so stupid, such an easy mark for Daryl's charms! If she'd kept her mind on her job and her hands to herself, she wouldn't be feeling like such a sucker.

First things first, she told herself. *Solve the case. Then you can kick yourself for being such a dummy!*

Bess broke into her thoughts. "What kind of stuff do you think Daryl was taking from the guy at the defense plant? Blueprints? Secret designs for bombs?"

"Probably," Nancy said. "And I'll bet it paid really well." Well enough, she figured, to keep gas in Daryl's Porsche and a grin on his face. "Daryl did it for the money, I'm sure, not for any political reason."

"I guess it beat bagging groceries after school," George commented. "Daryl must have thought he had it made."

"He did, until Jake found out," Nancy said. "It must have freaked him out, but he was so cool, you would never have guessed. What an actor!" Had Daryl been acting with her, too? she wondered. Coming on to her just so she wouldn't suspect him? She had to admit that that was exactly what he'd done, and she'd fallen for it! Well, she'd stopped falling, and now her eyes were wide open. "What I have to find out," she told the other two, "is who killed Jake. Was it someone from the compound or the man at the defense plant? Or was it Daryl? Or Hal or Walt or Connie?"

"Do you really think Daryl could have done something like that?" Bess asked.

"I'm just not sure," Nancy admitted. "But I have to find out. The question is how? I can't just walk up and—" she broke off suddenly.

"What is it?" George asked.

"Look who's here." Nancy pointed to Carla Dalton's table. Carla and the person she'd been with had stood up and were threading their way through the crowded room. Carla's companion was Brenda Carlton. They were headed toward Nancy.

"What's the ace reporter doing here?" George wondered.

"She'd better not be following me," Nancy said grimly. "We made a deal. If she messes me up, I'll take her reporter's notebook and burn it."

"Who's she with?" Bess asked.

"Oh, that's the famous Carla Dalton." Nancy laughed. "The one who likes to let people fall off trampolines." She giggled and then whispered, "I wonder what she'd say if she knew her ex-boyfriend was a spy?"

"She'd probably chew him out for being stupid enough to get caught," Bess joked.

As Brenda and Carla approached the girls' table, Brenda gave Nancy a sideways glance and a nasty wink. Nancy felt like throwing the last slice of pizza at her and watching the tomato sauce ooze down Brenda's black suede boots, but she held herself back.

Carla was chattering away about Bedford High's big dance as she and Brenda walked by, but she took the time to jostle the girls' table hard enough to spill Nancy's Coke.

Bess took a wad of napkins out of the container and handed them to Nancy. "Carla doesn't give up, does she?" she said, seething. "I don't understand why you haven't gotten back at her."

But Nancy had other things on her mind. Brenda, for one. *Had* she been following them? If she had, Nancy would have to be super careful. The case was at its trickiest point. She couldn't afford to let Brenda's nose for news get even a whiff of what was going on.

Then there was Daryl Gray. How was she going to handle him? "Of course!" she said suddenly. "Carla just gave me the answer."

"The answer to what?" George asked.

"How to get Daryl to spill his guts," Nancy told her. "Bess, you said Alan Wales is playing at the dance tomorrow night, right? So you'll be there, won't you?"

"Of course," Bess said dreamily. "I'm his biggest fan."

"Good, I might need your help." Nancy turned to George. "Yours, too."

"But I don't have a date."

"I've got one for you."

"I don't like blind dates," George protested.

"Trust me," Nancy said with a grin. "You'll love the guy I have in mind."

"So how are you going to handle Daryl?" Bess wanted to know.

"Very carefully," Nancy said. "But no matter what, tomorrow night, I'm going to pop the question to him. Only it won't be one he's expecting."

Chapter

Fourteen

Bᴇss sᴍᴏᴏᴛʜᴇᴅ ᴏᴜᴛ the skirt of her cherry-red dress and stood on tiptoe, trying to get a glimpse of herself in the mirror. "It's no use," she said with a sigh. "I'll have to wait until this place clears out."

"I'm not in any hurry anyway," Nancy said tensely. She and George and Bess were in the girls' bathroom just outside the Bedford High gym. It was the night of the high school's first big dance. For an hour and a half Nancy had been putting on an act—first when Daryl had picked her up at home, then on the drive to Bedford, and for the past forty-five minutes while she'd been dancing with him. She'd laughed and joked and made conversation, pretending that everything was the same between them. She probably deserved an Oscar for her performance, she told herself wryly. But staying in character was growing difficult. She'd been glad when the band had finally taken a break and she could take refuge in the bathroom and just be herself.

"Well, it won't be much longer," she said with a nervous glance at her watch. "I wish my hands weren't so clammy."

"Don't worry," George told her. "Daryl will just think you're excited to be with him."

"Speaking of that," Bess said, giggling, "what do you think of Alan Wales, Nancy? Isn't he absolutely gorgeous?"

"Incredible," Nancy agreed. Actually, she hadn't paid much attention to Bess's new heart-throb, but she didn't want to hurt her friend's feelings. "When this case is over, we'll all have to do something together."

"Oh, sure, that'll be great!" Bess said. "Of course, Alan's really serious about making it in the music business, so he's always busy. But we'll try to find a spare hour somewhere."

Nancy was glad Bess had a new boyfriend, but she just couldn't work up any enthusiasm for the subject, not at the moment, anyway. It wouldn't be long before she had to confront

Daryl, and that prospect was making her heart pound so hard it almost drowned out the sound of Bess's voice.

A girl behind Nancy finally moved away from the mirror, and Nancy grabbed the space. *Well, you don't look terrified,* she told herself. Actually, she looked good. She was wearing a dress she'd worn the year before, at a university dance with Ned—a soft blue wraparound that hugged her waist and came to a mildly revealing V in the front.

That V had put a sparkle in Daryl's eyes, but Nancy knew that the sparkle would fade fast once she started talking to him about Jake Webb, a man at a defense plant, and a diplomatic compound. What worried her was what would happen next. If Daryl was the murderer, would he turn on her? It was hard to imagine his getting vicious, but she knew it was a chance she had to take.

Nancy leaned close to the mirror to touch up her lipstick, and just as she brought the tube to her mouth, a girl moved into the space next to her, bumping Nancy's arm with her elbow.

Nancy stared at the pale red smear on the side of her mouth, and then at the girl who'd helped put it there. Carla Dalton.

George passed Nancy a tissue. Bess raised her eyebrows and shook her head. Nancy wiped her mouth and started over again. Carla ignored everyone, brushed her hair, and then turned to leave.

Suddenly there was a loud shriek, followed by a distinct thud. Carla was sitting on the bathroom floor, skinny legs sticking out in front of her, narrow lips pressed into a thin line of disgust.

Nancy was trying to figure out how Carla had gotten there, not that she cared, when Bess cried out, "Oh, I'm *so* sorry!" Her voice dripped with mock sympathy. "Me and my big feet! My mother always told me to be sure to keep my feet out of the way or people would trip on them, but I guess I just didn't see you coming." She shook her head and clicked her tongue. "Here, let me give you a hand up."

"Don't bother," Carla said through clenched teeth. "You've done enough!" She got clumsily to her feet and stalked out of the bathroom, but not before Nancy saw a large, soapy water stain smack on the rear of Carla's peach colored dress.

"Nice work. Thanks," Nancy whispered to Bess.

"Well, I just couldn't let her keep dumping on you," Bess giggled. "You've got enough on your mind."

George fluffed out her short dark curls and then checked her watch. "It's almost time," she said. "The band'll be back in just a couple of minutes."

Nancy took a deep breath. "You guys know what you're supposed to do, right?"

George nodded. "Don't worry. We'll be there." She grinned. "By the way, you were right about that date you got for me. He's terrific."

"I kind of like him myself," Nancy agreed with a laugh. "Okay, then," she went on. "I'll see you after the next break. Keep your fingers crossed." With another deep breath and a last look in the mirror, she walked out of the bathroom and into the Bedford High gym.

The band was just reassembling, and Nancy took a moment to try to relax before finding Daryl. The gym was decorated with hundreds of crepe-paper streamers, and colored spotlights sent shafts of red, blue, and orange to the floor. Nancy spotted Walt Hogan, looking happier than she'd ever seen him. She didn't see Hal or Connie, and she realized that Connie probably never went to dances. *Maybe when this case is over,* Nancy thought, *Connie will straighten her life out and stop trying so desperately to be somebody she's not.*

Alan Wales, the latest love of Bess's life, picked up his electric guitar and, with a frown of concentration, started in on a wild, pounding rock number that put everyone into motion.

"Okay, Daryl," Nancy said under her breath, "here I come, ready or not."

Her heart still pounding, Nancy threaded her

way through the crowded gym until she reached Daryl Gray's side. Without a word, Daryl grabbed her hand and pulled her close to him.

"Hey," Nancy joked, "this is a fast dance. I don't think I can move like this."

"Who wants to move?" Daryl whispered in her ear.

"I know what you mean." Nancy traced his lips with her finger and pretended to be feeling as passionate as Daryl was. "Let's just stick around a little while longer, though, okay? If we leave now, everybody will know why."

"I don't care about everybody," Daryl said with a grin. "But all right. As long as we're here, we might as well dance."

For almost half an hour, Nancy danced with Daryl. The band was good, keeping up a steady stream of popular rock numbers, as well as a few originals. They were all loud and fast, and it was almost impossible to carry on a conversation. Nancy was just as glad. She'd have to do some fast talking soon enough.

Finally, just before the next break, the band started in on a dreamy slow dance. Daryl took Nancy in his arms and held her tight, barely moving to the music. With a sigh he said, "This has to be the best night I've ever had."

This is it, Nancy told herself. She pulled her head back until she could look in Daryl's eyes. Touching his lips again, she whispered, "It could be a whole lot better, though, couldn't it?

Especially if we spent some time alone together. I've danced enough now. How about you?"

With a slow smile Daryl laced his fingers through hers and led her through the gym, around the slow-dancing couples, and out the door.

Nancy shivered as they crossed the parking lot, but it wasn't because of the cool night air. It was because the dangerous part of the evening was coming up, when Nancy would find out who Daryl Gray really was. Was he a nice guy gone wrong, or was he a killer?

Except for a few widely spaced lampposts, the Bedford High parking lot was dark, as Nancy had expected. Daryl's Porsche loomed like a black hulk in the shadows. Nancy forced herself to smile as Daryl unlocked the car and ushered her inside. As he walked around to the driver's door, she heard strains of music coming from the gym, and wished, for a second, that she were still at the dance.

Once Daryl got in the car, though, Nancy didn't have time to think of anything but his arms. They were around her immediately, and Nancy couldn't help remembering that just a few days before, she'd loved that feeling. She didn't love it anymore, but even as Daryl held her, she felt a pang of regret that such a gorgeous guy was involved in something so rotten.

Thinking of what Daryl had done, and might

have done, made Nancy pull away. "Hey," she said breathlessly. "Not so fast, there's plenty of time."

"I know, I know." Daryl was just as breathless. "I just love the way you feel." He leaned forward to kiss her.

Nancy put her arms around his neck, and when the kiss was over, she decided it was time. Bringing her lips close to his ear, she whispered softly, "I thought you'd like to know—I found out why Jake Webb was killed."

Chapter
Fifteen

For a second Daryl didn't move, and Nancy wondered if he'd even heard her. "Daryl?" she whispered again.

Finally, slowly, Daryl pulled away from her and sat back. In the faint light Nancy could see a look of surprise on his face. But fear was mixed with that surprise, and she knew that nothing was ever going to be the same between them again.

"Well," Daryl said. "Good work, Detective. How'd you do it?"

"I was lucky," Nancy admitted. "A piece of evidence was right in front of me, but I didn't see it for a while. It was on the tape."

"The tape? Jake's tape?" Daryl asked sharply.

"The one and only."

"Wow, you never know, do you?" Daryl gave a low whistle. "So which one did it?"

What an actor, Nancy thought. "It wasn't Hal or Connie," she told him. "It wasn't Walt Hogan, either." That was a guess on Nancy's part.

Daryl frowned. "But I thought you said you knew who killed Jake."

"No, I didn't. I said I knew *why* he was killed. There's a big difference."

Daryl shifted impatiently. "He was killed because he was blackmailing people and one of them finally stood up to him. We already know that."

"Yeah, that's true," Nancy agreed. "But it wasn't one of those three. They were all tucked in their beds when Jake took that fall." Nancy was still going on guesswork. For all she knew, Hal, Connie, and Walt could have formed a team and pushed Jake down the stairs on the count of three. But she didn't believe it, not for a minute. "So," she went on, "don't you want me to tell you what I found?"

"It's not exactly what I had in mind when we came out here," Daryl said, trying to joke, "but if you really want to talk instead of . . . doing other things, then go ahead."

"Okay, here's what I saw on the tape," Nancy said. "I call it 'The Daryl Gray Show.'" Calmly and quietly she went on to describe exactly what she and Bess and George had seen after Daryl had left her house that afternoon. *"Surprised* doesn't even come close to the way I felt when that tape ended," she said. "Sick is more like it."

Daryl didn't say anything, so Nancy kept talking. "But I was confused, too. I mean, I still didn't know what Jake had on you. So I decided to find out. I don't have to tell you where I went, do I? Out Route 110 to a U.S. defense plant. Then back to Bedford to a private estate where Russian diplomats hang out—relax, study a lot of top-secret plans from the defense plant, stuff like that."

Nancy shook her head and laughed softly. "I can just imagine how Jake felt when he realized what was going on. He must have thought he was sitting on a gold mine." She leaned forward slightly, and in the semi-darkness, she saw the expression on Daryl's face. He looked resigned, like a trapped animal that knows it can't get free. But like that trapped animal, he also looked angry, ready to strike out at anyone who came close.

For the first time since she'd left the dance with Daryl, Nancy felt she might be in danger. He was so close to her, physically, and she found herself wishing the Porsche were a little more roomy. Some space would be nice just then, the length of a football field, for example.

You're almost finished, she told herself. *Just get it over with.* "I know Jake told you that he'd found out your secret. I don't know how much of your 'salary' you had to fork over to keep him quiet, but that doesn't matter," Nancy said. "It probably didn't even matter to Jake after a while, because Jake decided to go after the bigger fish, didn't he? Which of your 'contacts' did he try to blackmail? The one at the defense plant? The one here in Bedford? Both?"

Daryl turned his head to look at her, and Nancy saw that the anger was growing stronger. "Well, it doesn't matter," she said. "I'll find out." She spoke quickly, wanting to finish before Daryl exploded. "What I really want to know—and what I think you can tell me—is who killed Jake. Was it you?"

The explosion came then. Nancy felt Daryl's hand—the touch of which had once made her quiver with excitement—close over her wrist in a painfully tight grip. Then he was getting out of the car, dragging her roughly after him. Nancy stumbled and felt her knee scrape the parking lot pavement, but Daryl had grabbed her arms by then, and was pulling her up and pushing her against the car.

"Listen," he whispered hoarsely, "Jake got in over his head, and so have you. If you think I'm a killer, what makes you think I'd stop with Jake Webb?"

Nancy saw the look of desperate fury in Daryl's eyes and knew she needed help. Fortunately she'd planned for it. As she stared back at Daryl, she saw his eyes blink suddenly as three sets of headlights were switched on in three different locations. The glare blinded both of them for a second, but Nancy heard car doors opening and knew that Bess and George were on their way. Most important, George's "blind" date—Ned Nickerson—was with them. Nancy was glad he'd come home for the weekend. Knowing he was there made her feel stronger.

Daryl heard the doors, too, and the sound of hurried footsteps on the pavement. He turned his head just in time to see the three figures moving swiftly toward the Porsche. Then he ran.

"Nan, are you all right?" Bess called out.

"I'm fine!" Nancy shouted back. She took off after Daryl, but before she'd taken even two steps, she felt someone rush past her. When she saw who it was, she stopped. Ned Nickerson could handle Daryl Gray any day of the week.

Ned's strong legs easily ate up the distance between him and Daryl. As Nancy watched he sprang into the air, landed on Daryl's back, and brought them both crashing to the ground. Then he was up, yanking Daryl to his feet. He half-dragged him back to the Porsche and slammed him up against its side.

"Ned!" Nancy had never seen him act so rough. When he'd arrived earlier, she'd told him everything about Daryl, except for his feelings about her—and vice versa. She was saving that for later, when the case was all cleared up. But seeing the tension in Ned's face, she wondered if he suspected something. She hoped not. She definitely couldn't handle it at the moment.

But then Ned loosened his grip on Daryl's jacket and turned to Nancy with an apologetic smile. "Sorry," he said. "I tend to get carried away when some killer threatens my girl-friend."

"Girlfriend!" Daryl exclaimed. Then he cried, "I'm not a killer!"

"You could have fooled me," Ned said quiet-ly, as he stepped away from Daryl and let Nancy take over.

"You didn't kill Jake Webb?" Nancy asked.

Daryl shook his head. "I just said that stuff to scare you off." His voice was drained of energy. He looked like a whipped puppy. "The guy at the defense plant—Mitch Dillon—killed Jake. He told me so." Daryl took a shaky breath and then went on. "See, Jake wasn't satisfied with blackmailing just me. So he forced me to get him in touch with Mitch. Mitch played along with him, let Jake set up a meeting at the school. Then he told Jake to give him the tape or he'd kill him." Daryl shook his head again, as if he couldn't quite believe it. "I don't have to tell you what happened then."

"Knowing Jake, he probably laughed at the guy," Nancy said.

"Yeah, and he died laughing, the stupid jerk." Daryl was calmer now. There was no anger in his voice, just sadness. "Anyway, when Mitch didn't get the tape he was ready to explode. He told me to get it, came on really strong with all kinds of threats."

"It was you in the video lab that day, wasn't it?" Nancy asked.

Daryl nodded. "I started to chase you," he explained, "but I just couldn't go through with it. I mean, what was I supposed to do when I caught you? Beat you up?" He smiled weakly and shrugged. "Waiting until you told me about the tape was one of the hardest times I've ever been through. But then when I watched it with you, I wasn't on it. I thought I could put this whole thing behind me."

Finally Nancy had the entire story. She should have felt like celebrating, but she didn't. She felt more like crying. From the looks on Bess's and George's faces, she could tell they felt the same way. How could you celebrate when someone—even a creep like Jake Webb— had been murdered? When Daryl Gray's life was probably ruined?

Nancy glanced at Ned. As usual, he sensed how she felt before she had to tell him. He came over and put his arm around her shoulders. Nancy smiled at him and then turned back to Daryl.

"I don't think you'll ever be able to put it behind you," she told him. "Not completely, anyway. You'll have to face up to what you've done, and to what the government will want to do to you."

Daryl didn't bother to answer. He just gave a defeated shrug, not meeting her eyes.

"But I think I know a way for you to make it a whole lot easier on yourself," Nancy went on.

Daryl raised his head, a spark of interest in his beautiful eyes. "How?"

"By helping us catch the murderer."

"You've got to be kidding! Mitch has nothing to lose at this point." Daryl's eyes swept over the parking lot, as if he were trying to find an escape route. But he was trapped, and he knew it. "Don't you understand?!" he screamed. "He'll kill me!"

Chapter

Sixteen

Ned turned the car smoothly onto Bedford Road, heading toward the high school. Then he glanced over at Nancy, who was frowning in concentration. "Do you really think Mitch Dillon would kill Daryl?"

"I just don't know," Nancy admitted. "Who can say for sure?" She felt uncomfortable just thinking about it. On Friday night, in the parking lot, she'd spent almost forty-five minutes convincing Daryl to see things her way. By helping her put Mitch Dillon behind bars, she'd said, Daryl would be easing his conscience. And it might help him out of some of the trouble he'd gotten himself into. She'd told

Daryl that *he* didn't have much to lose, either. It had been easy enough to say then, when she was persuading Daryl to go along with her plan.

But Monday was three days later, and in a few short hours, they'd be putting that plan into action. It was a good plan, Nancy knew, but no plan was foolproof. And if something went wrong, Daryl would be the one to pay the price.

Sensing her worry, Ned reached over and squeezed her hand. His classload was light for the next few days and he'd decided to stay and help out. "Hey," he said gently. "Everything's going to be fine. I'll be there. George and Bess and Alan will be there. Even the police are coming. And you're way ahead of the game, where they're concerned. You've already solved the case and they're still scratching their heads about it."

"Well, I had a head start on them, plus a very important piece of evidence." Nancy began to feel better. "Besides, I do need them. They're the only ones who can make an arrest."

Nancy giggled, remembering the look on the police captain's face when she'd told him her story. He'd never heard of Nancy Drew, girl detective, and it took two phone calls—one to her father and one to Mr. Parton—to make him stop looking angry and start looking amazed.

Once he got over his amazement, though, the captain had been more than willing to go along with Nancy's plan. It was a simple plan, really.

Daryl had called Mitch Dillon, told him he had the incriminating tape, and set up a meeting with him for Monday afternoon at five-thirty. At the meeting Daryl would make sure that Mitch talked about murdering Jake Webb. The best part of the plan was that Nancy and her friends were going to get the confession on videotape, using a hidden camera.

As Ned drove toward Bedford High, Nancy checked her watch. In a few hours the case would be over, she hoped. The thought of having to wait out the entire day in school was driving her crazy. But she wanted to keep an eye on Daryl and make sure he didn't bolt. She didn't think he would, but she couldn't take that chance.

"Now, remember," Ned joked as he pulled the car to a stop, "don't lose your lunch money and don't cut any classes."

"Very funny," Nancy said. "How about if we trade places? You go to school and I'll scout around the meeting place?"

"No, thanks. But I will make a deal with you." Ned leaned over and put his hand on the back of her neck. "You behave in school and our trip to the mountains will be next weekend. Mom and Dad are dying to get up there. The cabin has a big stone fireplace, and it's really cozy on cold nights."

"You've got yourself a date!" Nancy bent her head and kissed Ned, wondering how she'd ever thought Daryl Gray was exciting. But she had, and she was going to have to deal with that sooner or later. Later, she told herself. She gave Ned another lingering kiss, then hopped out of the car and went in to school.

If Nancy really had been a student, she would have flunked out for sure. At least ten times that day, she'd been caught staring out the window instead of taking notes, and her English teacher had come right out and asked her if she'd left her brains at home. "Where is your mind, Miss Drew?" Nancy was tempted to tell him that her mind was on blackmail, espionage, and murder, but she kept her mouth shut. He would probably have sent her straight to the school psychologist.

She saw Daryl twice—in the hallway and in the cafeteria—and he seemed fine. Nervous, but ready to go, he said. Nancy was nervous, too, and edgy with waiting, but knowing that Daryl was holding up okay made her relax a little.

The next time she saw him was at the meeting place, a public park near Bedford High. She'd joined Ned, Bess, Alan, and George there as soon as school was out. Ned had been exploring the park most of the afternoon, finding the best place to conceal the camera. He was showing Nancy some heavy shrubs that looked perfect, when Daryl came running up to them. Nancy glanced at his face and felt her heart begin to sink. Daryl looked terrified.

"It's Mitch, he . . ." Daryl gasped for breath. "He called me at school, pretended he was my father. We—we can't go through with this!"

"Why not?" Nancy asked. "What did he say?"

"He said he can't make it at five-thirty," Daryl told her. "I don't know if he suspects anything, but he's going to be here in ten minutes, and there's no time to let the police in on the change of plans!"

Nancy felt a moment of panic herself, but in just a few seconds, that panic changed to anger. "Look," she said, "maybe he does suspect something, he wouldn't be a very good spy if he didn't keep his eyes open. But he can't possibly have any idea about what we've got in store for him. We can't just give up. He could be planning to leave the country or something. This might be our last chance to get him!"

"Nancy's right," Ned said quietly. "Besides, if Daryl doesn't show, then Mitch will definitely suspect something."

It was too late to try to do any more persuading. Nancy just looked at Daryl, silently urging him to hang in. Daryl stared at the ground a few seconds, considering. Then he raised his head and nodded at Nancy. "Let's go, Detective."

As calmly as if they had an entire police force

waiting in the wings, the six young people took their places. Bess and her rock star-to-be sat close together on one of the park benches, their arms around each other. They didn't have to pretend to be in love, Nancy noticed.

Nancy, Ned, and George concealed themselves behind the shrubs, where they could film the encounter without being seen. Nancy panned the camera over the park, stopping on Daryl for a few moments.

Daryl was sitting on another bench, some distance away from the young lovers. Nancy had been worried about him before, but as she looked at him now, the worry vanished. He was lounging casually on the bench, idly scanning one of his school books, looking as calm and relaxed as the day she'd first seen him at the stoplight in Bedford.

"He's pretty cool," George commented softly.

Nancy nodded. "He really missed his calling. He should have been an actor." A branch was poking her in the ear; she reached up to push it away and felt Ned's hand close over hers. She smiled and started to say something, but just then Ned's eyes shifted from her face and she felt him tense. "Company," he whispered.

Through the camera lens, Nancy watched a heavyset man stroll into the park. He was wearing jeans and a dark-blue windbreaker, and as he stopped by the duck pond, he brought out a handful of popcorn from his pocket and threw it into the water. He didn't hurry or glance around. He was simply a man taking a late-afternoon walk through the park.

Just one thing set him apart and made Nancy's hands begin to sweat—his bushy mustache. It was the same mustache she'd seen on Jake's tape, and he was the same man who'd met Daryl in front of the defense plant. It was Mitch Dillon, spy, killer, and soon-to-be convicted criminal, if everything went the way Nancy hoped it would.

Dillon stopped feeding the ducks, and as he walked along the curved path at the edge of the pond, Nancy could tell that he wasn't as oblivious to his surroundings as most people would have thought. His eyes roved constantly over the park, looking for signs of a trap. As he glanced over the shrubs where the camera crew was hidden, Nancy instinctively held her breath, even though she knew he couldn't see her.

Then Dillon took a drink from the water fountain, and when he straightened up, he gave the surroundings one last look. Seemingly satisfied, he wiped his mustache and began a slow amble toward Daryl.

Nancy gripped the camera tightly, holding it steady as Dillon eased himself down on the bench beside his "contact." Nancy saw Dillon's lips move; then Daryl nodded, reached into his bookbag, and pulled out a bulky envelope. It wasn't the incriminating tape, of course; it was blank. Daryl didn't hand it over right away, though; instead, he started talking, and Nancy knew he was talking about Jake Webb.

Keep talking, she urged Daryl silently. *Get that murder confession out of Dillon and onto that mini-cassette you're wearing under your shirt.*

Nancy hated being where she was, out of earshot, looking at the scene through a tiny lens. She wanted to be where the action was, hearing everything for herself. It was frustrating, being so out of it. She toyed with the idea of giving the camera to George or Ned and sneaking through the bushes until she was closer to Daryl and Dillon, but she decided it wasn't worth the chance. One false move, one too many twigs snapping under her feet, could blow it. And she couldn't afford to blow it, especially without the police to back her up.

Dillon reached for the envelope then, but Daryl didn't let go. He was still talking. That must have meant that Dillon hadn't said anything about Jake's murder. Nancy wondered why. Could something have gone wrong? Was Daryl being so obvious that Dillon suspected something?

Keeping the camera steady, Nancy looked away from the viewfinder for a second. Maybe a "real" look would tell her something. But before she could see anything, a blinding flash of light went off in the bushes in front of the park bench. Nancy stared long enough to see Mitch Dillon leap up from the bench, the envelope in his hands. Then she dropped the video camera and began running. Something had gone wrong and Dillon was on his feet. Nancy had to stop him before he got away!

Chapter

Seventeen

As Nancy raced through the bushes a scream rang out, shattering the peaceful silence of the park. There was another scream, and then a woman's voice cried, "What are you doing? Let go of me!"

Although the shrubbery blocked Nancy's view, it didn't matter. She would have known that voice anywhere. It belonged to Brenda Carlton. The "ace" reporter had blown it for Nancy again.

Nancy was so angry she was shaking. Mostly she was angry at herself. She'd made the deal with Brenda, and she should have known better. Brenda couldn't be trusted; she was trouble, right down to the tips of her perfectly manicured nails. Thinking about Brenda made Nancy careless for a second, and a second was all it took. A thick root lay like a snake across the path; Nancy tripped on it and went sprawling face down, right next to the bench where Daryl and Mitch Dillon had been sitting.

"Well, well, who's this?" Dillon said with a sneer. "Another member of the kiddie corps? Get up!" he ordered roughly.

Nancy stood up, quickly appraising the situation. Daryl was standing a few feet from the park bench, Brenda's camera and its flash attachment on the ground in front of him. Dillon had one arm around Brenda's neck, and in his other hand he held a gun. The gun was pointed at Brenda's head.

"Nancy, please," Brenda stammered. "I didn't mean for this to happen. If—if you'd just told me everything, I would have stayed out of your way!"

"You've been following me the whole time, haven't you?" Nancy said.

Brenda nodded dumbly and then winced as Dillon tightened his grip around her throat. Brenda's eyes were terrified, and Nancy couldn't help feeling sorry for her. There was no pity in Mitch Dillon's eyes, though. They were about as compassionate as a shark's. "That's enough chitchat, girls," he said. "It's time to stop playing games."

"This isn't a game," Nancy said.

Dillon eyed her coolly. "You're right, it's not. It's real life and it's going to get rough if you don't do what I say." He shifted his glance to Daryl. "I want that camera," he said, eyeing Brenda's camera on the ground. "You hand it to me and nobody gets hurt. I'll walk out of the park and out of your lives. It'll be like a bad dream."

It already is, Nancy thought. Her mind was racing, trying to figure out what to do. Then suddenly she noticed something—Bess and Alan were close by, but neither Ned nor George had followed her through the shrubs. So Dillon had no way of knowing that they were even around. Nancy knew Ned and George well enough to know that they weren't just standing by, waiting to see what happened. One of them had probably snuck out of the park already and called the police. If Nancy could keep Mitch Dillon talking, keep him from leaving somehow, then there was a chance they could get out of the mess. All she needed was time. "What happens if you don't get the camera?" she asked.

Dillon sighed wearily. "If I don't get the camera, then somebody gets hurt. Do you want to guess who?" He spoke as if Nancy were a child asking annoying questions, and Nancy decided to play along with him.

"Who?" she asked.

"Who do you think?" Brenda cried. "I'm the one he's pointing the gun at! Will you just give him the stupid camera so he'll let me go?!"

"Smart girl," Dillon said. "I suggest you follow her advice, Red."

Nancy hated to be called Red, especially by someone like Dillon. "And if I don't, then you'll kill her, just like you killed Jake Webb, right?" she asked.

"You're catching on fast," Dillon replied. "I already killed one nosy kid. I'm not afraid to kill another. You got it just right."

At least we got the confession, Nancy told herself, *no thanks to Brenda.*

Dillon shifted impatiently. "Now, how about the camera, Red?"

Nancy gritted her teeth. "If you want it so much, why don't you get it yourself? Nobody's stopping you. We're all just a bunch of stupid kids, remember?"

"You may be stupid but I'm not," Dillon said. "You think I don't know what'll happen if I reach for that camera? You'll try to play hero and jump me, and even though I'd win, I just don't have time for a brawl right now."

"I'll bet," Nancy said. "Gotta catch a plane to Russia, right? Back to the U.S.S.R."

"I'm starting to lose my patience." Dillon shook his head in disgust and turned to Daryl. "Okay, buddy. Do your partner one last favor and hand me the camera. Now!"

"Don't do it, Daryl!" Nancy shouted.

"Nancy!" Brenda squeaked. "What are you doing? He's going to kill me!"

"That's right." Dillon was staring at Daryl. "I'm going to kill her if you don't give me that camera in ten seconds. Ten . . . nine . . ."

"Hey." Daryl held out his hands. "Just keep cool, Mitch. I'll give it to you."

"Six . . . five . . ."

Brenda opened her mouth, but no sound came out.

"Four . . ."

Slowly Daryl bent down and took hold of the camera strap. As Dillon reached the count of two, Daryl straightened up and in one quick move swung the heavy camera at Dillon's face. At that same instant the gun went off.

The gunshot set Nancy into motion. She didn't know if Dillon hit anyone, but she hurled herself at him, determined to stop him from doing any more damage. She hit him just below the knees, and as she tried to get a good grip on his jeans, Dillon reached down and took a swing at her. His fist collided with her jaw in a punch that gave her an instant headache.

You really do see stars, Nancy thought. Her ears were ringing and her vision was blurred. It was hard to tell exactly what was going on, but she sensed a lot of movement around her. Then she heard a familiar voice calling to her. "Don't worry, Nancy!" Ned shouted. "The police are on their way!"

Nancy rubbed her eyes and saw Ned and Alan racing together after Mitch Dillon, who was charging across an open field of grass, heading for the sidewalk that bordered the park. He was still clutching the fake tape in one hand, and the camera swung wildly by its strap in the other.

If Dillon had only known that neither the tape nor the camera was going to do him any good, he might have gotten away. But he was determined to take all the "evidence" with him, and it slowed him down. The heavy camera kept banging into his knees. It probably hurt, Nancy thought with satisfaction, which was why Dillon finally broke stride for a few seconds and tried to get a tight grip on the camera itself.

Those few seconds were all it took. As Dillon grappled with the camera, Ned and Alan put on a burst of speed and reached him just as he was about to take off again. First Ned, then Alan leaped on top of Dillon, the three of them rolling over and over until they came to a jarring stop against the base of a water fountain. Dillon wasn't going anywhere for the moment; they had him. Nancy closed her eyes in relief.

When she opened them again, the first person she saw was Brenda Carlton, looking more like a bag lady than a fashion-conscious reporter. Her butter-soft leather boots were covered with mud and grass stains, her red silk blouse was missing two buttons, and a smear of lipstick decorated her chin. She was still sitting where Dillon had tossed her; the gun was right next to her, and every time she looked at it, she sobbed hysterically.

A hundred sarcastic remarks went through Nancy's mind, but before she could decide which one to say, Bess touched her shoulder. "Nan?" Her voice was shaky. "Do you know anything about gunshot wounds?"

"What?" Nancy whirled around to face her friend. "Were you hit?!"

"No, I'm okay," Bess assured her. "It's Daryl."

Daryl Gray was sitting a few feet away from Brenda. His handsome face was pale, and his eyes were full of pain. He was clutching his right shoulder, and even as Nancy looked a bright red stream of blood seeped through his fingers.

"I don't think it's too bad," he said as Nancy crouched beside him. "But it sure does hurt."

He grinned weakly, and Nancy smiled back. "Thank you," she said. "You really came through for us."

"So did this," George said triumphantly. She emerged from the bushes and pointed at the video camera she was carrying. "I got the whole scene on tape, every last bit of it!"

Nancy gave her a thumbs-up signal for victory, and at the same moment she heard a police siren, faint at first, but growing louder by the second. It was all over. They'd done it, and Nancy laughed, barely feeling the pain in her swollen jaw.

Chapter

Eighteen

WHEN NANCY WALKED into Mr. Parton's office the next afternoon, the principal stood up and gave her a smile that seemed to light up the entire room. The confused, worried look had left his eyes, and there was a definite spring in his step as he came around the desk to shake her hand.

"Your father told me you were first-rate," he said, beaming at her. "I'm glad I listened to him."

"Thank you," Nancy said with a laugh. "I'm glad you did, too." She sank into a chair and took the mug of steaming tea Mr. Parton offered her.

"How do you feel?" the principal asked. "I understand you made 'direct contact' with Mitch Dillon's fist."

Nancy touched her jaw. There was a purple bruise on it that her makeup didn't quite cover, but she decided it went with the territory. "It only hurts when I laugh," she joked. "Anyway, it was worth it to see the police handcuffing Mitch Dillon." By the time the police had arrived at the park, all the fight had gone out of Mitch. He'd listened in stony silence as his rights were read to him, but Nancy could see the panic in his eyes. He was finished, and he knew it.

"Murder and espionage." Mr. Parton whistled softly. "Right here in Bedford. If Jake Webb hadn't been so greedy, it might still be going on." He shook his head in amazement. "Well, Dillon won't be busy for a long time, that's for sure."

"What about his foreign contact?" Nancy asked.

"I don't suppose we'll ever get the whole story," Mr. Parton said, "but I heard on the news this morning that two 'diplomats' checked out of their Bedford mansion last night. Mother Russia probably wanted them home fast."

"I guess that takes care of the spy ring, for a while anyway," Nancy said. "What's going to happen to Daryl Gray?"

Mr. Parton's good spirits took a dive for a

moment. "I don't know yet." He sighed. "He's in deep trouble, no doubt about that. I still can't believe he did what he did."

Nancy agreed, but she felt strongly that Daryl deserved a break. "I know you feel terrible about him," she said, "but I think if it hadn't been for Daryl, Mitch Dillon would have escaped yesterday. Daryl did the right thing in the end. He also got shot for it."

Mr. Parton nodded. "You're right. And I'm sure the government will agree with you. He'll have to pay for what he did, but maybe the price won't be so high." He sipped some tea and relaxed again. "By the way, the police are holding Jake's videotape for evidence, but they've promised to keep as quiet as they can about Walt and Hal and Connie."

"That's great!" In spite of what they'd done, Nancy couldn't help feeling that those three kids had been victims as much as anyone else. "Have you talked to them?"

"To all three," Mr. Parton told her. "Hal's taking the SATs again, Walt decided to bench himself for a while, and Connie's agreed to get some help for her shoplifting problem. So there's a happy ending after all. And," he went on, "I didn't mention your part in the case, even though I wanted to."

"Good. Who knows?" Nancy said. "I might have to come here undercover again someday."

Mr. Parton winced and then shook hands with her. "Don't take this the wrong way," he said, "but I hope not!"

As Nancy took a last walk through the halls of Bedford High, there was a spring in her step, too. She had solved the case, but it was more than that. She caught sight of Hal and Walt and Connie and noticed that all three of them seemed to have lightened up overnight. In fact, the whole atmosphere of the school had lightened up. Maybe since the biggest secret had been revealed, the smaller secrets—injury and cheating and shoplifting—could be forgotten.

A lot of kids were carrying copies of *Today's Times,* and Nancy noticed that Brenda Carlton had finally gotten her name on a front-page story, beneath the headline BEDFORD POLICE CRACK ESPIONAGE RING. Nancy smiled to herself as she picked a copy of the discarded paper off the hall floor. Brenda must have been very happy to keep her part of the bargain and leave Nancy's name out of the story.

As Nancy quickly scanned the article, she saw with relief that Daryl's part in helping catch Dillon got just as much play as his role of courier for spies. Brenda, naturally, didn't mention her own near-disastrous actions at all.

Daryl was still in the hospital, the story said, but was expected to recover quickly. Nancy had a feeling that he could always bounce back, and she was sure that in a few years he'd get over the nightmare he'd been involved in.

So things were turning out okay, she thought as she pushed open the door and walked outside. She had just one loose end to tie up, and then she could put the Bedford High case behind her and move on to the next one, whatever it might be.

The "loose end" was Ned Nickerson, and he was waiting for her in his car. *This is as good a time as any to tell him about Daryl,* Nancy thought. She pulled her jacket collar up against the chilly October wind and went down the steps to meet him.

"Hi!" Ned pushed open the door for her and took her hand as she slid in. "Did everything go okay?"

"Fine," Nancy said, and told him what Mr. Parton had told her.

"Great. Then it's all over, huh?"

"Almost." Nancy linked her fingers with his and took a deep breath. She wished she'd had a chance to discuss her problem with Bess, but there hadn't been time. Besides, Bess was so involved with Alan Wales that she was hardly paying attention to anything that was going on around her. She and Alan ate, slept, and breathed guitars and musicians. Nancy was on her own. After another deep breath she said,

"Ned, there's something I have to talk to you about."

"I bet I can guess," Ned said softly. "It's Daryl Gray, isn't it?"

"You mean you knew?"

"Not really," Ned told her. "But I saw the way he looked at you a couple of times. And the way you looked at him."

Nancy should have guessed. Ned knew her better than anyone else. "It wasn't much, really. I mean we didn't fall in love or anything like that. I guess we were just attracted to each other. I wasn't looking for it to happen, it just did."

"You don't have to explain," Ned said. He stared ahead of him, at the entrance to Bedford High.

"But I want to!" Nancy squeezed his hand and tried to get him to look at her. "I feel terrible telling you, but it's better than keeping it from you. Because I love you," she said. "No other guy could be as perfect for me as you are."

"Then it's over?" Ned asked.

"It hardly got started," Nancy said.

"So there's nothing to talk about, is there?" Ned finally looked at her, but Nancy couldn't read the expression in his eyes. She couldn't tell what he was thinking.

"I guess not," she said. "But I wanted to tell you anyway."

"I understand. I'm glad you did." Ned pulled her close and kissed her gently. "Let's get out of here, okay?"

"Okay!" Nancy kissed him back and settled herself in the seat. She was glad she'd told him, too, but had she done the right thing? Ned said he understood, but did he, really? Would she have understood if he'd told her about some girl at the university?

Nancy shook her head, trying to get rid of such disturbing thoughts. It was over. She'd done what she thought was right, and she'd just have to wait to see what happened.

As the car pulled away from the school, Nancy turned and took one last look. It was a handsome, modern building, and it appeared peaceful in the afternoon sun. It was hard to believe the things that had gone on behind its red brick walls.

Nancy turned and caught Ned's eye. He was smiling at her and she felt a sudden urge to run her fingers through his hair. She also felt relieved that she'd told him the truth about Daryl. She didn't want any secrets between her and Ned. She'd found enough secrets at Bedford High.

Nancy's next case:

When she investigates a rock star's mysterious disappearance, Nancy once again finds herself probing perilous secrets! Her only lead takes her straight to Bess's new boyfriend. What is he hiding? Finding out may kill her friendship with Bess. But *not* finding out may kill the kidnapped rock star—with Nancy and her friends next on the hit list.

THE NANCY DREW FILES™

Case 2

Deadly Intent

Carolyn Keene

Chapter

One

COME ON, BESS, cool it," Nancy Drew whispered. "People are starting to stare."

But Bess Marvin seemed not to hear her best friend's voice. "I just can't believe it!" she gushed. "It's all too much! New York City, Radio City Music Hall, the Bent Fender concert . . ."

"The hottest rock band around," said Alan Wales, Bess's latest boyfriend. "And they've invited us backstage!"

"Oh, George, help me with these star-struck kids," teased Nancy. "I think your cousin has gone off the deep end."

"Well, you have to admit, this *is* going to be

1

one incredible vacation," George Fayne said, falling in step with the group.

"The best," Nancy declared, running a hand through her reddish-blond hair. "And no mysteries, just fun. This detective needs a little break."

At eighteen, Nancy had already earned a reputation as one of the nation's top young detectives, solving mysteries all across the country, and overseas as well. Her most recent one, though, *Secrets Can Kill*, had started in a high school just a few miles from her hometown of River Heights.

"Well, maybe you need a break, Nan, but *I* can think of one mystery I wouldn't mind solving," Bess spoke up.

George threw her cousin a puzzled look. "Since when are you into detective work?"

Nancy was puzzled, too. George was always eager to jump right in and help her on a case, no matter how dangerous, but Bess usually had to be coaxed. Unraveling mysteries scared her, and she was the first to admit it.

"Yeah, what mystery do you want to solve?" Nancy asked.

Bess giggled. "The mystery in Barton Novak's big green eyes," she answered. "I wonder if he's as gorgeous in real life as he is on MTV."

"I should have figured." George let out an exasperated sigh. "You're not planning on doing anything to embarrass us in front of him and the rest of the band, are you?"

"Yeah, don't go getting any ideas," joked Alan, pulling Bess closer to him.

"Hey, guys, don't worry. One guitarist is enough for me." Bess stood on tiptoe and gave Alan a kiss.

In the few weeks since they'd met, Bess and Alan had been inseparable—joined at the lip, Nancy liked to joke. They reminded her of the way things used to be between her and Ned Nickerson.

Nancy found herself wishing for those days. But then, it had been her own choice to get involved with Daryl Gray during her last mystery. And although it was over with him almost before it started, she couldn't blame Ned for feeling miffed. Since then, she had visited Ned once at Emerson College, and he had come to River Heights for a weekend, but things had been cooler than usual between them, and that hurt. She could only hope they could put the past behind them.

"Nancy Drew! Earth to Nancy!" Bess tapped the top of Nancy's head. "Anyone home up there?"

"Sorry, Bess. What—?"

"I said that of course Alan's my number one guitarist, but it *is* pretty incredible that we're going to meet Barton Novak in a few seconds, isn't it?"

Returning to the exhilaration of the moment, Nancy smiled. She remembered the thrill she'd felt listening to Bent Fender and how she'd followed their rise from struggling performers to top stars.

Alan echoed Bess's enthusiasm. "I've memorized practically every song Barton's ever recorded. The first thing I ever figured out how to play on my own was the lead for 'Break Down the Walls.'" He moved his hands, playing imaginary notes on an air guitar. "I'm so psyched that you guys are taking me along tonight!"

"Alan, how could we not take our favorite future rock star to meet our favorite current rock star?" Nancy smiled and gave him a light punch on the arm. "Besides, Dad said the musicians in the band were happy to have us all."

Nancy's father, a lawyer, was negotiating the band's new recording agreement. Normally, Carson Drew worked on criminal cases. But Bent Fender's drummer, Roger Gold, was the son of his old college roommate, Sy Gold, who had recently moved to a town not far from River Heights. He and Nancy's father had rekindled their old friendship, and now Carson Drew was doing Mr. Gold a favor by working on the contract for his son's band. In return, Roger and the band were letting Nancy and her friends come backstage for one of their concerts, and they were going to give them a personal guided tour of the New York rock clubs.

"What a mob scene," Nancy said as she and

her friends edged through the crowd of noisy fans in front of the Music Hall. Off on one side of the building, Nancy caught sight of a polished brass door.

"This is it, the stage door!" she exclaimed, mounting a few steps and pushing the door open. Just inside, in a glass booth, sat two burly security guards in identical tan uniforms.

"Hi," Nancy said. "Roger Gold told us to come back and see him before the show."

The bearded guard frowned wearily. "Young lady, do you know how many times we've heard that one?"

"But it's true," Nancy insisted. "His father is a friend of my father's. He's expecting us."

The guards exchanged glances. "Why don't you kids give us a break?" the other one said. "There have been at least a dozen folks in here already, trying to get to see the band. We—"

"Roger said you'd page him when we arrived," Nancy interrupted, remaining polite.

The guards exchanged another glance.

"Listen," Nancy persisted, "I'll make you a deal. You let Roger know Nancy Drew and her friends are here, and if he doesn't want to see us, we'll leave. I promise."

The guard with the beard shrugged and picked up the telephone.

"Way to go, Nan," whispered George.

A few seconds later, the guard was hanging up the receiver, an apologetic look on his face. "I really thought—I mean, so many kids come back here—"

"No problem," Nancy said. "You were just doing your job."

"He said he'll meet you downstairs."

The guard pointed to the elevators. "Jeez." He scratched his head. "I could have sworn you were just another bunch of crazy fans."

"We are," Alan called back as they headed for the elevators. "But we're a lucky bunch of crazy fans!"

Nancy laughed. Alan had hit the nail on the head. From the moment she'd heard Bent Fender's first single, she'd been hooked. And now she was about to get a behind-the-scenes look at one of their concerts. It wasn't just any concert, either. It was the first of Fender's 'Rock for Relief' shows, a series of benefits to aid handicapped children.

A wave of excitement washed over Nancy as she and her friends got into the elevator. She smoothed her hand over her short, electric blue skirt and picked a thread off her oversized sweater. Her long, lean legs were flattered by a pair of patterned tights, which looked perfect with her favorite ankle boots.

"Don't worry. You look great, as usual," Bess told her. "You too, George," she added, eyeing George in the simple black jumpsuit that hugged every line of her athletic body. "Boy, what I would give to be able to wear an outfit like that."

"You look pretty fabulous yourself," George returned. "I love that turquoise shirt with your blond hair."

"You don't think it makes me look too fat?"

"No way," Alan said. "You look perfect." He was wearing tight jeans and a T-shirt, the picture of a rock-and-roller. Bess reached up to tie a turquoise bandanna around his neck.

"Same color as your shirt," George grinned. "Looks like you're color-coding your boyfriend."

The elevator door slid open, and the friends stepped out. There, looking just as Nancy had pictured him, stood Roger Gold, unmistakable with his spiky black hair and single silver earring.

"Hi," he said easily.

There was an uncomfortable silence as Nancy and her friends studied the legend standing before them.

Roger smiled at each of them in turn, his gaze finally coming to rest on Alan. "Well, *you're* not Nancy," he joked.

Nancy took a step forward. "No, I am," she said, not quite believing that she was talking to a superstar like Roger Gold. "And these are Bess and George and Alan." She indicated each of her friends in turn.

"Hello," they chorused nervously. Nancy saw how tongue-tied they looked.

"Nice to meet you all," Roger responded. Then he said, "Nancy, I've been hearing stories about your father ever since I can remember. My dad claims they were the best roommate team in the history of college life."

"Yeah, my dad says the same thing." Nancy was still a bit awed by Roger's presence. Although Barton Novak's name was almost synonymous with Bent Fender, Nancy had always felt most loyal to Roger. After all, their fathers had been best buddies. Nancy had not met Roger before, since he had grown up with his mother outside of Los Angeles, but she'd known about him long before he'd become a star.

"Did your dad ever tell you about the time he and my dad got into the kitchen at the dining hall—" Roger began.

"—and colored the mashed potatoes purple," finished Nancy. She laughed, loosening up. Roger was so open and friendly that he made it easy to remember that stars were people too. "And how about when they had that ten-foot-long submarine sandwich delivered to their history class?"

"Yeah. That's one of my dad's favorite stories," Roger said. "So where is your father, anyway?"

"Back at the hotel, getting ready for the opera. He's not too big on what he calls 'that music you kids listen to.'" She gave an embarrassed shrug.

"Hey, don't worry about it. Your dad told

Barton and me that he wasn't into rock when we talked to him about our contract. To each his own." Roger hesitated. "Hey, listen, let me introduce you to the rest of the band. They're in the lounge having a little preshow Ping-Pong match. Linda's our resident champ. She's wasting Barton."

Nancy saw George's face light up at the mention of Linda Ferrare, Bent Fender's bass player and backup vocalist. George was a great fan of Linda's tough, powerful voice and dynamic style.

Roger led them to the lounge and pushed open the door. There, at one end of the Ping-Pong table in the center of the room, stood Barton Novak, his brow creased in concentration beneath a shock of blond hair. Bess let out an audible sigh. Barton snapped his paddle as the ball came toward him. On the other side of the table, Linda prepared to return the shot. She slammed the ball so hard it went speeding out at a crazy angle, bouncing at the very corner of Barton's side of the table. He took a wild swing and missed.

"Game," said Linda, tossing her curly dark hair.

There was a smattering of applause from the rest of the band members. Mark Bailey, the other guitarist, was sitting in an armchair; Jim Parker, the keyboard player, was on the couch.

"Nice shot." Barton wiped his forehead. Then he looked toward the door for the first time. His expression lightened up. "Hey, gang, we've got guests. Hiya."

"Guys," Roger said, "this is Nancy Drew. I was telling you about her. And these are her friends, Bess, Alan, and Georgia."

"George," she corrected.

"Sorry." Roger grinned. "So, all of you, say hello to Mark, Jim, Linda, and Barton." Roger pointed to each person, but Nancy had studied Fender's album covers enough to know the band members instantly.

"Thanks for inviting us to come tonight," Nancy said to them.

"The pleasure's ours," Barton replied gallantly. "We get to have the hottest detective around at our show tonight."

Nancy could feel heat rising to her cheeks. Barton's face had been on the cover of *Rolling Stone, Time, People,* and half a dozen other major magazines, and he was complimenting *her.* "I am beginning to make a name for myself," she said humbly.

"Beginning? From what I hear, you've done it." He looked at Nancy. "If you don't mind, I'd like to talk to you after we're finished playing tonight." Nancy cocked her head. Did she detect a note of urgency in Barton's voice?

"I'd be glad to," she said, trying to read his expression. But if he was worried about something, he gave no further clue. Instead he joined in the enthusiasm of her friends.

"This is a dream come true for me," Alan blurted. "I'm Fender's biggest fan. And I've learned a lot by listening to you," he said to Barton.

"You play guitar?"

Alan nodded. "I mean, I'm no—well, no Barton Novak." He grinned. "But I'm getting better all the time."

"Do you play in a band?" Jim Parker wanted to know.

"The Mud Castles," Alan answered. "We've been getting gigs in some clubs and bars around River Heights."

"The Mud Castles?" Roger turned to Alan and studied his face closely. "Hey, you know, I think I heard you when I was visiting my old man a few months ago. Did you play a bar over in the South End—Puffy's or Puffer's or something?"

"Puffin's. Yeah, that was us. But how come we didn't recognize you?"

"I had on dark glasses and a hat," Roger said, almost apologetically. "It's nice to be able to go out like a regular guy once in a while, have a couple of beers. But I had to leave when someone at a table near the bar started giving me funny looks. I just didn't want to hassle with anyone figuring out who I was."

Nancy tried to picture Roger in her hometown bar, rubbing elbows with people she'd known all her life.

"Yeah, I like that little place," he went on.

11

"And Alan, your band was terrific. You play lead, right?"

Alan nodded.

Roger turned to his fellow band members. "This kid is okay." He jabbed his finger in Alan's direction. "More than okay. Someday he'll put us out of business if we're not careful!"

The smile on Alan's face could have lit up the entire room. Nancy flashed Bess a thumbs-up sign.

"We'll be out of business sooner than you think," Linda interjected, "if we're not on stage in half an hour." She looked at Nancy and the others. "Make yourselves comfortable. Play some Ping-Pong or something while we get ready."

"We'll be back soon," Barton Novak broke in, "and then we'll take you out to the wings to watch the show."

Nancy grinned. She sensed that this night—this rock concert—would be special.

George was going for the game point twenty minutes later when the lounge door burst open. The ball flew by unheeded as Roger Gold appeared in the doorway.

"Show time?" Nancy asked excitedly, putting down her Ping-Pong paddle. Then she saw the worried expression on Roger's face as his eyes darted around the room.

"Barton's not here?" Roger was trying to

sound calm, but Nancy could hear the edge of panic in his voice. His hands were clenched, knuckles white, on the doorframe.

"What's wrong, Roger?" she asked.

"Barton's disappeared. I've looked all over the building, and he's gone."

"Disappeared?" George finally caught the bouncing Ping-Pong ball. "Maybe he just went out to get some air."

"Five minutes before we go on? No way!" Roger took a deep breath. "I've got a bad feeling about this. Real bad."

Chapter

Two

Nancy stood in Barton's dressing room with her friends and the rest of Bent Fender. On the vanity lay uncapped tubes and containers of stage makeup. An open can of Cherry Coke was almost full. A guitar was leaned up in the corner of the room, next to a portable amplifier.

"It looks like he was right in the middle of getting ready," Nancy said. "Not like he planned on going anywhere."

"You're sure?" Roger asked.

"There's no question about it," Nancy replied grimly, bending down to look under the vanity. A pair of cowboy boots—the ones the rock star always wore on stage—sat on the floor.

"Barton had these on when we were introduced to him before. That means—"

"—that wherever he is, he's barefoot," George finished.

"Exactly. That's why I don't think he intended to leave this room."

"You mean he was just sitting here, and then . . ." Bess's voice trailed off.

"Something happened. Maybe someone knocked on his door and he got up to answer it." Nancy thought out loud, trying to piece the puzzle together. She felt herself switching gears, the excitement she'd experienced at meeting her rock idols melting into the clear, quick thinking that had earned her her reputation as a detective.

She pulled open the door to the little dressing room, just as Barton might have done. Across the corridor was a rehearsal studio for the Rockettes, who danced in special shows at Radio City Music Hall. Lights from the street washed through the room, glinting off the mirrors lining one wall. The hallway between the two rooms was littered with stage props and lighting equipment.

Nancy stepped out of the room to inspect the jumble of boxes, painted scenery, and other theater paraphernalia. "Hey, you guys, come look at this." A few yards down the hall, the contents of a box of lighting gels was scattered every which way. A papier-mâché tree trunk

15

nearby was broken in half. "Looks like a scuffle," Nancy noted.

"Here's something else," Bess observed. A broken lamp lay on the floor down the hall.

"Wow! There's a whole trail of things!" Nancy said.

"I don't know, Nancy," Linda Ferrare spoke up. "We've performed in a lot of places, and it's not that unusual for the backstage or storage areas to be a jumble of stuff like this." She paused, and her voice dropped. "Besides, I think there's something you ought to know. It's been kept quiet because we don't want the press to find out. But this isn't the first time."

"I don't understand." Nancy surveyed the trail of clues. "Has Barton vanished before?"

"Not exactly." Mark Bailey spoke up. "A few years back—twice—he just took off. We were scared stiff at first because he didn't tell anyone anything, but both times it turned out that he just couldn't cope with the pressure of being a super-celebrity. The first time he flew off to some island in the Mediterranean and rented himself a house on the beach for a few weeks. The second time he spent the weekend with some friends in the country."

"Yeah, but Mark, don't forget, that was two years ago," Roger said, "when we were just starting to make it big. Barton's gotten much better about dealing with his fame." A worried look crossed his face. "I just don't have the same feeling about this."

"Why not?"

"Look," Roger said, "this whole 'Rock for Relief' thing was his idea. I know he's pretty quiet about his sister, but he's totally devoted to her. You know that. He wouldn't let her—or anyone like her—down."

"What does his sister have to do with it?" Nancy asked.

"She's been in a wheelchair all her life," Roger explained. "That's one of the reasons Barton got the idea for these shows. I'm positive that he wouldn't run out on us now. Besides, if he were planning on going, he wouldn't have left all that stuff in his dressing room. Even his guitar is there."

Jim Parker ran a nervous hand through his short dark hair. "But he's got two other guitars, Roger. I don't know. Barton's done some crazy things."

Nancy listened carefully. Barton was beginning to be a real human being to her, with fears and weaknesses like any person. If he had chosen to vanish before, she had to consider the possibility that he might do it again. On the other hand, there was evidence to the contrary.

Nancy sighed. "I can't begin to make guesses about someone I've just met, but I'm inclined to agree with Roger. Vanishing just before a big show like this doesn't make sense and isn't going to be overlooked by the press. If Barton wanted to get away from it all, he couldn't have picked a worse moment to do it."

"Look, everything you're saying sounds reasonable," Linda volunteered, "and it's true that Barton's become more comfortable being, well, being a hot item, but just recently he's been a lot more like the old Barton. I don't know, he seems really uptight about something."

Nancy couldn't help thinking about the urgency she'd sensed when Barton had asked about her detective work. "Linda, do you have any idea what was bothering him?"

Linda shrugged. "Beats me. But he's been acting weird for the past couple of weeks. Ever since . . ."

"Ever since what?"

"Ever since we started talking about our new contract." Linda's olive complexion went pale. She glanced from one member of Bent Fender to the next. "You don't think he's going to leave the band, do you?"

"No way, Lin," Roger reassured her. "Look at the way he's been going at the songs he's writing for the new album. He's totally into the music we're making now." Roger paused. "But he has been tense about the contract." He turned to Nancy to explain. "He thinks we're not getting all the royalties we're entitled to. He started fighting with our agent and our producer. That's why we called your father. We decided to bring in a lawyer."

Nancy nodded. But before she could ask more questions, the telephone in Barton's dressing room rang shrilly.

Mark grabbed the receiver. "Yes?" Pause. "Hey, thanks for calling. Have you found him yet?" His expression darkened, and Nancy held her breath. "Right. Okay, I understand."

"That was the stage manager," Mark said when he hung up. "No trace of Barton, and the audience is getting pretty rowdy. They want to know why we're not on stage. What do we do?"

Jim shook his head thoughtfully. "Whew. All those handicapped kids are out there. We can't let them down."

"Yeah, but how are we supposed to play without the main attraction?" Linda asked, her tough tone barely hiding the concern in her voice. "Boy, if this is Barton's fault, I'm going to make him disappear for good."

"I could cover the leads," Mark said, "but can you imagine doing 'Fever' with one guitar?"

" 'Fever?' What a great tune. I can play every riff in that song," Alan said.

Roger spun around and looked him squarely in the eye.

"Hey, I'm sorry." Alan looked at the ground, embarrassed. "At a time like this I guess no one wants to hear me go on about playing your music."

"No, maybe we do," Roger said, studying Alan intently. "Can you play all our tunes?"

"Well, yeah."

"Really well," Bess added proudly. "He has a great voice, too."

Roger grabbed Barton's guitar from the corner of the room and fiddled with the knobs and dials on the amp. "Try the fast middle section on 'Fever.'" He pressed the guitar into Alan's hands.

Astonishment filled Alan's brown eyes. Roger flashed him a smile of encouragement. "Go ahead," he said.

Nancy listened as Alan tuned the guitar strings and, after taking a long, deep breath, sang the familiar Fender music in a clear, confident voice.

"Not bad." Linda's face was serious, her eyes appraising. "What else can you do?"

"How about 'Little Brother'?" Jim asked, as Alan finished up on 'Fever.' "Do you know that one?"

Alan's brow crinkled in concentration. "That's an oldie," he said, "but I think I can do it." Once again, music filled the room as Alan broke into a slow, dreamy number from Bent Fender's first album.

"What do you say?" Roger addressed his fellow band members. One by one, Nancy saw them signal their approval.

"Champ," Roger said, putting his hand on

Alan's shoulder, "how would you like to be our pinch hitter tonight?"

As if in a fog, Alan put down the guitar. "Me? You want *me* to play with Bent Fender? *Here?*"

"We need your help," Roger said.

"We'll pull you through the rough spots," Mark promised.

Nancy watched as Alan's angular features reflected a rainbow of emotions from doubt to dazed happiness. Then the smile left his face. "What about Barton?" he asked suddenly. "Are you going to call the police?"

"They wouldn't take this seriously," Roger replied gloomily. "Not after the other two times. Barton's earned himself quite a reputation."

"But you can't just do nothing," George said.

Nancy cleared her throat. Despite seeing her dreams of vacation vanishing as rapidly as Barton had, she said, "Look, maybe I could—"

"Nancy, *would* you?" Roger didn't even wait for her to finish her sentence. "I can't tell you how grateful I'd be."

Linda, Jim, and Mark echoed his sentiments.

"Nancy Drew can't turn down a chance to do some sleuthing," George said. "It's in her blood to track down clues."

Nancy had to admit that George was right. Nothing was more of a challenge than solving a mystery. But just then, the tingle of enthusiasm that she usually felt at the beginning of a case was overshadowed by her worries about Barton. Maybe he *was* running away again, but if not, she couldn't lose any time. He might be in terrible danger.

As she combed the halls of the renowned Radio City Music Hall, Nancy could hear strains of the concert coming from the direction of the stage. Alan's playing wasn't as slick or polished as Barton's, but from what Nancy could hear, his fingers were really flying over Barton's guitar. The rest of the band was helping Alan out by covering more of the leads themselves and taking more solos. Still, Alan was winging it like a true pro.

Nancy wished she could be in the wings watching, but finding Barton came first. Bess and George had offered to help her, but she insisted they enjoy the show, telling them she would come get them if she needed their help. Bess, in particular, had looked relieved, obviously not wanting to miss a single note of Alan's performance.

The sounds of the concert grew clearer as Nancy entered an elevator, pressing the button for the street level. When the elevator door slid open and she headed for the guards' booth, the music grew faint again.

The guards and some of Fender's roadies were playing cards. But the bearded guard she had met before looked up from his hand when Nancy asked about Barton. "Novak hasn't shown yet," he said.

"And you haven't seen anyone back here besides the people with the band?"

"The only folks I let in—besides you and your friends—were these guys here," he pointed to the three card-playing roadies, "the gal running the lights, the guy at the sound board, the stage manager, and the two who were unloading equipment before the show."

"What two?" One of the roadies, a lanky, fair-haired young man, put down a can of beer and shot the guard a puzzled look. "We unloaded all the equipment this morning."

The guard frowned. "You're off the wall," he snapped. "Those guys had passes, and they were carrying boxes and stuff."

"They weren't with *us,*" another roadie declared.

Nancy drew in her breath. "Sounds like trouble." She opened her shoulder bag and took out a felt-tipped pen and the tiny notebook she always carried with her. "Tell me everything you can remember about those guys," she said.

"One of 'em was real big—tall with brown hair," said the bearded guard. "How was I supposed to know they didn't belong here? And those boxes—they looked like they had instruments in them, you know—"

"Guitar cases?"

"Yeah, I guess. And they had a huge brown

box, too, looked like the kind that refrigerators are packed in. Actually, they left with that one. Said they were taking out a broken speaker."

Nancy's heart sank, a terrible thought occurring to her. "Was that box large enough to hold a person?"

"I don't believe it!" exclaimed the blond-haired roadie, throwing down his cards. "Did you let some thugs carry Barton out of here in a box, you morons?"

"Please!" Nancy shouted. She got the group calmed down and continued to pump the guards for information about the two unknown men. "Was the tall man's hair straight?" she prodded. "Curly?"

"Straight. Not too much of it, I don't think. I sort of remember a bald spot. And he was a heavy fellow. Dressed in jeans and a jeans jacket."

"What about the other one?" Nancy said.

"Younger. Your age, maybe. Shorter, but he looked strong. Dark wavy hair. Longish. Parted on the side. He had on slacks."

"Gray ones, I think," put in the other guard. "And a button-down shirt. Oh, and he had on a heavy gold chain and a gold ring. I noticed the ring when he showed us their passes. Real different-looking, like a sea serpent or something, and it had little red jewels for eyes."

"That's terrific," Nancy said. "Thank you.

Anything else you can think of that might help me?"

"Well," one of the guards said slowly, "we *have* had a little trouble around here lately—break-ins, equipment missing, that sort of thing. But I don't see what that would have to do with Barton."

"All right," said Nancy. "Well, you've been a big help."

"Now what are you going to do?" the roadie asked.

"I want to take one more look around and make sure I didn't miss anything."

Nancy didn't discover anything more in the basement or on the street level. The rehearsal studios were dead ends. But as she poked around near Barton's dressing room, she spotted two black instrument cases. She'd seen the cases earlier and thought nothing of them, but because of her talk with the security guards, she raced over and unlatched them. Empty. They'd probably been carried in just so the two mysterious men would look as if they belonged backstage.

Nancy poked at one of them. It moved slightly, and she noticed something new—a fat wallet. She picked it up, turning it over in her hand. The wallet was made of soft, top-quality leather, decorated on one side with a tooled design of a dragon, its tail curled into the letter L. It was bulging with money.

Nancy ran her finger over the raised leather. Suddenly she remembered the guard's description of the gold ring one man was wearing. He had said it was shaped like a sea serpent—but couldn't the sea serpent have been a dragon?

Eagerly, Nancy opened the wallet to see what other clues she could find, but just as she did she heard a noise behind her. She whipped around and felt a dull thud on her head. It was the last thing she remembered before everything went black.

Chapter

Three

THE BACK OF Nancy's head ached when she woke up. Her fingers discovered a large bump, and she rubbed at the soreness. It was then that she recalled being struck. She blinked hard, pulling herself to her feet. The walls around her seemed to spin, and she put her hand out to steady herself.

From the direction of the concert hall came the sound of applause, stamping feet, and cheering fans. Was the show already over? That would mean she'd been out for at least an hour. Taking a few deep breaths, she tried to clear her head. Then she remembered the wallet.

She looked on the floor, under the instrument

cases, behind pieces of scenery, inside boxes of props. The wallet was gone. "What on earth is going on?" she whispered in frustration.

"Nan? Did you say something?" George appeared around the corner, followed by Bess, Alan, and the members of Bent Fender.

"Did you find out anything about Barton?" Roger called to her.

"Did you hear Alan? Wasn't he incredible?" That was Bess.

"Did you miss the whole concert, Nancy?" asked Linda.

"Hey, one person at a time," Nancy replied weakly. Her friends' faces looked blurry.

"Nancy, are you okay? Is something the matter?" George asked. She and Bess rushed to Nancy's side.

"I'm not sure. I found something—that much I know. A wallet. But just as I was taking a look at it, someone hit me over the head, and I blacked out. When I came to, the wallet was gone."

"Someone knocked you out?" Bess's voice was a frightened whisper. "Do you know who did it?"

Nancy shook her head. "Maybe the same people who have Barton. Or maybe just some creep who wanted the wallet. It was full of money, and the guard said there have been some break-ins recently."

"But you said somebody might have taken Barton." Roger Gold's voice trembled.

"Well, I think so. Two men were back here before the show . . ." Nancy told them everything she had found out. "I want to look around a little more," she said, finishing up. "Maybe that wallet wasn't the only thing around that might tell us something. *Ouch.*" She put her hand to her aching head.

"You're not looking for another thing tonight," George told her firmly. "You've got some bump there. We're putting you right to bed and getting you an ice pack."

"But George . . ."

"Your friends are right," Linda said. "In fact, it might be a good idea to have a doctor take a look at you."

"I'm all right, really," Nancy insisted, but as she spoke, the hall began to spin and she felt her knees weaken. She reached out to lean on Bess's shoulder.

"Nancy, the doctor is a good idea," Bess said.

"But if there are other clues . . ."

Roger spoke up. "We'll have the security guards search every inch of this place and report back to you if they find anything out of the ordinary."

"Well, okay," Nancy agreed grudgingly. She did feel awfully woozy.

She let the band members put her and her

friends in a taxi to the hotel, but not before promising them that she would be back on the case first thing in the morning.

At the hotel, the house physician gave Nancy a clean bill of health, much to everyone's relief.

Carson Drew had arrived home from the opera to find his daughter in bed in the luxurious suite they were sharing. An ice pack rested on her head, and Dr. Harris was bending over her.

"Dad, you should be getting used to my misadventures by now," Nancy joked weakly.

But the tight lines around Carson Drew's mouth did not soften even after the doctor announced that his daughter was going to be as good as new in the morning. Nancy knew that her father worried about her.

"You go right to sleep and get a solid night's rest," Dr. Harris told Nancy. "That's my prescription."

Nancy nodded sleepily. Once she was alone—her friends in their own suite, her father in the next room—she tried to go over the evening's events in her mind. But she was thoroughly exhausted. Try as she might to stay awake for just a few minutes longer, she felt herself drifting into a deep, dreamless sleep.

"Sleeping beauty," Bess giggled.

"Shh. You'll wake her up," George whispered. "Let's just leave the tray."

"But the omelet will get cold," Bess protested.

"Bess, you know Dr. Harris said she needs rest."

Nancy rolled over and pulled at the quilt that covered her. She opened one eye. Her friends were setting a breakfast tray on the table in the corner of the room. "S'all right, you guys," she mumbled, still half asleep. "I'm getting up."

"Nan! Good morning, sleepyhead." Bess flounced down on the edge of the bed. "How are you feeling?"

Nancy pulled herself into a sitting position, leaning against the backboard of the king-size bed. She checked the bump on her head and found that the swelling had gone down. "Pretty good." She looked around the hotel room. "Hey, it's nice in here, huh?" She hadn't had a chance to look around much when they'd checked in, and after the concert nothing could have been farther from her mind than the hotel room.

"Yeah, and get a load of the view," George said, pulling open the curtains to reveal the skyline of New York's midtown, sparkling in the early-autumn morning sunshine.

"The Empire State Building!" Nancy noted enthusiastically.

"And that other one is the Chrysler Building," Bess informed her. "One of the bellhops told us all about it. Boy, you should have seen him. He was really cute!"

"Bess, honestly," Nancy kidded. "I thought Alan was enough for you."

31

"Well, I only noticed 'cause I thought maybe George—"

"Thank you very much, cousin dear, but I think I can take care of myself," George interrupted her.

"You guys . . ." Nancy laughed. "Hey, what's on the tray? I'm starved. Whoever gave me that smack on the head did me out of an after-the-show supper."

"Nancy, that's not funny," George said. "You could have really been hurt."

"George, I'm fine. If you should worry about anyone, it's Barton Novak." Nancy grew serious. "Speaking of whom, is there anything new on him?"

George held up a newspaper. Four-inch headlines were splashed all over the front page. Nancy could read them from across the room. ROCK STAR VANISHES, the headlines screamed. "That's the latest," George said. "He still hasn't turned up, and nobody's heard from him."

Nancy pushed off the covers and jumped out of bed. "Time to do some investigating."

"Wait," George protested. "Aren't you even going to have breakfast? We brought it up here for you, and you said you were starved."

"This is more important."

"Nan, I really think you should eat something. You can't miss meals if you're going to start running around the way you do on cases." She brought the breakfast tray to Nancy's night table.

Bess looked longingly at the scalloped potatoes and cheese omelet. "I wish I could put away a breakfast like that and not gain any weight," she said. "You don't know how lucky you are, Nancy."

Nancy sat back down on the bed and took a big bite of a croissant. "All right. You two win." She ate quickly, not tasting much, wanting to get to work as soon as possible. "By the way, where's my dad?"

"He went out jogging. The woman at the front desk told him about a trail in Central Park. He looked in on you before he left, but you were sound asleep. He told us to keep an eye on you." George joined Bess at the edge of Nancy's bed.

"Oh." Nancy wolfed down a few bites of omelet. "I was hoping he could take me over to meet Bent Fender's agent. I know he was planning to see her about their contract this morning."

"Well, he ought to be back soon," Bess said. "But what do you want to talk to that agent for? You think she knows something about Barton?"

"Roger said Barton was fighting with her about their royalties. And with their producer, too. I think that's where I have to start." Nancy took a last swig of orange juice and pushed her tray away.

"Finished?" asked Bess, helping herself to the remaining half a croissant and the last few bites of the potatoes.

At that moment, the door to the hotel suite opened, and Carson Drew stepped in, wearing a navy blue jogging suit and running shoes, his salt-and-pepper hair pushed away from his face with a sweat band.

"Hi, Dad. Did you have a good run?"

"Very nice. Lots of company. I think half the city must be out jogging in the park this morning. How are *you?*" he asked, planting a sweaty kiss on Nancy's forehead.

"Raring to go." Nancy got out of bed and opened her suitcase, taking out her favorite black jeans and a hot pink oversized shirt. "In fact, I wondered if you would mind bringing me with you to Bent Fender's agent this morning. I'm hoping she might be able to give me some information about Barton. Did you see the headlines about him?" She held the newspaper out for her father to look at.

Carson Drew nodded. "I read the article. The media really have a field day when something happens to a big star. They didn't have anything substantial to report, though. Well, perhaps Ann Nordquist can help. I'm meeting her—" Carson Drew checked his watch, "—in forty-five minutes," he said as he headed for his room.

Nancy showered and got dressed quickly. "Do you guys want to meet me for lunch later?" she asked Bess and George. She was whisking on a light dusting of blush and pulling a brush through her hair.

"Sounds good," George said. "How about you, Bess?"

"Can't." Bess shook her head. "I told Alan I'd meet him at the record producers'. Then we'll go out for lunch, just the two of us."

"The same producers who handle Fender?" Nancy shot Bess a quizzical look.

"Yeah. Alan's gone to talk to them about getting a recording contract." Bess was almost exploding with joy. "Nancy," she said, "I know you didn't get to hear him last night. He was incredible! This is the start of something really big. I can just picture screaming fans all around, begging for Alan's autograph, trying to get a glimpse of him, to see him smile—and he'll wade through the crowd and climb into the limousine that's waiting for him." Bess smiled impishly. "Of course, I'll be in the back seat." Bess opened up the locket she always wore around her neck and studied Alan's photograph.

"Don't you think you might be getting the teensiest bit carried away?" Nancy asked gently, trying to avoid jolting Bess out of her fantasy. "I know Alan's got a lot of talent, but only the biggest groups record on the World label. They don't go with unknowns."

"Nan, after last night, Alan is *not* an unknown. They even mentioned him in that newspaper article."

"Okay, Bess, but don't be disappointed if they don't sign him right up. Remember, last night was his first major show, and his job was really to imitate Barton's playing as closely as possible."

"I'm not worried."

George caught Nancy's glance and arched a troubled eyebrow.

"Ready, Nancy?" Carson Drew called.

"Ready," Nancy replied distractedly, her mind on Bess and Alan. She slung her bag over her shoulder. "See you guys," she said, taking one last worried look at her friend as she left. When, she wondered, would Bess's bubble burst?

Chapter

Four

NANCY AND HER father entered the twenty-third-floor office of Ann Nordquist's agency. The walls were papered with posters of foreign places.

"I love to travel," Ms. Nordquist explained, after Carson Drew had introduced her to Nancy and explained that Nancy wanted to speak to her for a few minutes. She ran a perfectly manicured hand through her pale blond hair. "I just got back from a tour of mainland China. And the first thing that happens is—that." Ann Nordquist gestured to the day's newspaper Nancy had brought along. "It's awful, isn't it?"

"Yes, it is," replied Nancy. "In fact, that's why I'm here. Ms. Nordquist, Roger Gold told me that you and Barton had been, well, quite frankly, having some problems working together. Something about royalty money."

A tiny frown appeared on Ann Nordquist's forehead. "I wouldn't exactly say we were having problems. You have to understand that royalty revenue is a complicated business. It goes through many channels and often takes some time before it ends up in the artist's pocket. I don't think Barton quite understood that. He felt he was getting shortchanged."

"And he wasn't?"

"I don't think so, not unless something irregular is going on at World."

"They're my next stop," Nancy said. "Maybe you could tell me the names of the people there who handle Barton and Bent Fender."

"Certainly. In fact, I'll make a list for you." The agent reached for a piece of paper, and Nancy studied the attractive woman as she wrote. She had a pleasant, straightforward manner, and she seemed open enough. But Nancy wondered whether there was more to her disagreement with Barton than she'd let on.

"Here you are." Ann Nordquist pushed the list toward Nancy, a half-dozen names written out in her neat, round handwriting. "I ought to warn you about Harold Marshall. He's not the easiest man to deal with."

"Well, I'll try my best," Nancy said. She and Ann Nordquist chatted with Carson Drew for a few minutes, Ann confirming some of the things the members of Bent Fender had said about Barton—that he tended to be publicity shy, and that he had indeed picked himself up and vanished on two occasions without telling a soul.

"That makes finding him all the more difficult," Nancy told her, "because if he has been kidnapped, there are going to be plenty of people who won't believe it."

"Like the little boy who cried wolf," Carson Drew supplied.

"Exactly." Nancy stood up to go. "Well, I'll leave you two to do your business. Ms. Nordquist, thank you for your time."

"You're welcome. I hope you can track Barton down quickly. We're all awfully worried about him." Ann Nordquist extended her hand to Nancy. "I hope next time we'll meet under more pleasant circumstances."

"I do too. By the way, would any of the people on this list fit these descriptions? A tall, heavyset man with straight dark hair, but balding slightly. Or a shorter man with dark wavy hair, possibly wearing a gold ring in the shape of a dragon or sea monster?" Nancy looked up from her notes on the two men who had been seen backstage.

Ann Nordquist thought for a few seconds. "I don't believe so. No." She shook her head.

"Okay. Well, thanks again." Nancy said goodbye and walked the ten blocks to World Communications' offices. Normally, she would have been thrilled to be on the streets of New York, watching the stream of people and window shopping, but that day she walked quickly, her mind on Barton Novak as she weaved through the crowds. Had he been kidnapped, as Roger Gold suspected, or had he gone on his own, as the rest of the band seemed to think?

Soon, World Communications loomed up in front of her, an imposing steel and glass tower with uniformed guards at the door. *Not again,* Nancy thought, recalling the guards at Radio City Music Hall. She prepared a little speech, but was surprised when the guards let her in with no trouble. In fact, though she found out no new information about Barton, the people at the company were happy to answer her questions. That is, until she got to the last person on the list Ann Nordquist had given her—Harold Marshall.

She opened the door with his name on it and found herself standing before a stylish, sharp-featured young woman of about her own age. The woman's dark hair gleamed with henna-red highlights, and her blue sweater was cut low in the front.

"Yes?" The woman looked up from her desk.

"I'd like to see Mr. Marshall, please." Nancy smiled.

The young woman did not smile back. "Do you have an appointment?"

"No, but I'd like to speak with him about Barton Novak."

"Barton?"

"I'm investigating his disappearance."

"Mr. Marshall is a very busy man, Miss—"

"Drew. Nancy Drew." Nancy extended her hand.

The young woman barely touched it. "I'm afraid he's all booked up today."

"Could it be that he has something to hide?" Nancy suggested, surprised at her own brazenness. When she got no response, she moved toward the inner door and pushed it open.

"Hey, what are you doing? You can't go in there!" the secretary announced, following behind.

"I've already done it," Nancy replied. She found herself facing a small, wiry man with a brown mustache and glasses, who was sitting behind an enormous desk. "Hello, Mr. Marshall."

"Who are you?" He released a cloud of noxious cigar smoke as he spoke. "Vivian, what's she doing here? I gave specific instructions that—"

"I'm sorry, Mr. Marshall," Vivian said, her voice taking on a honey-sweet tone, "but she barged right in here. I couldn't stop her. Please don't be angry."

Harold Marshall's expression softened for a split second. "Oh, Vivian, of course it's not your fault. I didn't mean to snap at you." Nancy watched him. "But as for you—Miss Drew, did you say?" His expression changed to a sneer as

41

he turned back to Nancy. "What is so important that you felt you could waltz right in here? First, my office is invaded by an idiot who thinks that just because he banged out a couple of Barton Novak's riffs last night we must be dying to cut a record—"

"Alan?" Nancy groaned out loud. So poor Alan, filled with dreams of glory, had come face to face with Harold Marshall. Nancy's heart went out to him and to Bess.

"You're a friend of his? Look, I told him no dice, and I mean it. Now, if you'll excuse me . . ." Marshall swiveled around in his chair.

"I am a friend of Alan's, but that's not why I'm here. I'm a detective, and I must ask you a few questions about Barton Novak. Ann Nordquist said you handle his band."

Marshall spun back around, puffing on his cigar. "Ann Nordquist is a pushy dame."

"You mean you don't handle Bent Fender?" Nancy asked.

"I didn't say that. Oh, all right. Go ahead and ask your questions. But be quick about it. I have more important things to do than chat away the morning with someone who calls herself a detective."

Nancy felt her face flush with anger, but she tried to stay calm. "Mr. Marshall, suppose you tell me everything you can about Barton's disappearance."

"Disappearance! Hah!" he snorted. "I hate to

disappoint you, Miss Drew. I know how excited you must be about solving this mystery." His voice oozed sarcasm. "But Barton Novak is safe and sound."

"He is?" Nancy's emotions were a confused jumble of astonishment, relief, and disbelief. "What do you mean?"

"Publicity." George Marshall pronounced the word as if it were an explanation in itself.

"I don't understand."

"It's a publicity gimmick. News like this is certain to boost sales on Fender's most recent album. It's been done plenty of times before. Remember the rumor after the Beatles released *Abbey Road?* That Paul McCartney had died? No, you were probably in diapers back then."

"I *do* know what you're talking about," Nancy countered. She couldn't imagine a rock-and-roll fan who hadn't just about memorized the history of the Beatles. "The record buyers kept thinking they saw clues about it on the album cover and in the lyrics to the songs, isn't that right?"

"The girl detective gets an A plus," Marshall said snidely.

"So you mean Barton's disappearance was engineered?" Nancy shook the newspaper in anger, the realization of what Marshall had done washing over her like a tidal wave. "Why didn't you tell anyone? The rest of the band members are either furious or scared stiff about him."

"Hey," Harold Marshall drawled. "That anger

and fear bought us four-inch headlines. If we'd told them, their reactions wouldn't have been so . . . real." He allowed himself a satisfied smile.

"That's a rotten, inhuman trick," Nancy exclaimed.

"Kid, this is business. What counts is what sells records." Marshall shrugged. "Those fans are going to go wild when they think Barton's gone. They'll start looking for clues in the records, the rock videos. . . . All teens think they're detectives, as you well understand," he added condescendingly.

Nancy bristled. "What I understand is that you think it's good business to lie to Bent Fender's fans. Either that, or to lie to me."

"Look, Miss Drew, if you don't believe what I've told you about Barton, that's your problem. Anybody find a ransom note?"

"No," admitted Nancy, fighting back the urge to grab the mug of coffee on his desk and fling it in his face. "But couldn't you tell the rest of Bent Fender where Barton is, just for their own peace of mind?"

"Let's get something straight." Harold Marshall's lips thinned. "We're sitting on a publicity gold mine here. I only told you what's really happening so you'd stop wasting my time. If you go to the press with anything I said, I'll deny it. Who do you think they'll believe—me, or some kid playing detective?"

He stared at Nancy, challenging her. "As for

Barton, he's a big boy. He could call the band members to tell them he's okay—if he wanted. Maybe he wants some privacy. Think of this as kind of a vacation for him. And do us both a favor. Keep your mouth shut about this whole business."

Nancy didn't like Harold Marshall's tone, but she had to admit to herself that what he was saying jived with everything she'd heard about Barton's thirst for privacy. "Maybe," she said. "But wasn't it strange to pull off this stunt right before the biggest of the 'Rock for Relief' concerts?"

"More publicity that way. Now, if we're all finished here, you can show yourself out."

Nancy took a few steps toward the door, where Vivian, who had stood there all the time, put an insistent hand on Nancy's arm. The interview was clearly over.

"Oh, just one more thing, Mr. Marshall." Nancy turned in the doorway. She asked if he'd ever seen the two men described to her by the Radio City guard.

Marshall shrugged. "How am I supposed to keep track of everyone who goes in and out of this place?"

Did I expect any other answer? Nancy asked herself, leaving Harold Marshall's office without further conversation. She found her way back to the elevator banks, rode down to the main floor, and walked past the indoor fountain and the greenery that adorned the lobby, into the crisp midday sunshine.

Her head swam with conflicting thoughts as she made her way back to the hotel to meet George for lunch. Harold Marshall was one of the rudest, most self-important people she had ever met. But he was just the kind of person to cook up a sneaky publicity trick like the one he'd described. And the fact that no ransom note had been received would suggest that Barton hadn't been kidnapped.

But what about the two mysterious men at the Music Hall and all the clues Nancy had discovered outside Barton's dressing room? Marshall's publicity scheme didn't explain them.

And it didn't explain something else, Nancy thought. *That attack on me last night was no stunt. It was serious—deadly serious.*

Chapter

Five

"GEORGE, CAN YOU think of any reason why Harold Marshall would want his biggest star out of the way?" Nancy asked, helping herself to a breadstick.

"How do you know he's not telling the truth?" George held down her napkin as a breeze drifted across the outdoor table at the café where the two girls were having lunch.

"I *don't* know. That's the trouble. It's so confusing. But George, even if Barton isn't in trouble, I'm absolutely convinced that something fishy is going on." Nancy rubbed the back of her head as proof. "But how am I supposed to know where to look when I don't even know what I'm looking for?"

"You tell me, Nan. You're the detective."

"All I do know is that Harold Marshall is creepy. Poor Alan, getting his dream shattered by that goon."

"Well, someone was going to do it sooner or later. That concert last night really put stars in his eyes. I mean, he's acting totally blind as far as realistic expectations go." George leaned over sideways to allow the waiter to put down a bacon cheeseburger in front of each girl and a basket of french fries between them. "Thank you," George said, reaching for a fry. "Anyway," she continued, "Bess isn't helping matters. The way she's been talking, you'd think Alan was going to be the next Bruce Springsteen."

"Well, it's pretty obvious that Harold Marshall cleared up that misconception quickly."

"Mind if we join you?" Nancy heard a familiar voice behind her. She turned around to find Bess and Alan, both smiling broadly.

"Hi! What are you guys doing here? Bess, you said you and Alan were going to have lunch together somewhere."

"We were, but we stopped off at the hotel first and got the most incredible news. We just had to tell you. The hotel manager said he'd recommended this place." Bess plopped down in an empty seat beside Nancy. Alan sat next to George.

"So what's happening?" Nancy asked, noting the looks of pure happiness on their faces. She was more than ready to hear some good news.

"They've decided that—" Bess and Alan both began speaking at once.

Bess laughed. "You go ahead and tell them, Alan. It's your news."

"Well, Vivian from the record company called," Alan said breathlessly, "and they've decided they want me to cut an album for them!"

"What?" Nancy couldn't believe what she was hearing. "But I saw Harold Marshall after you did and he said . . ." Her voice trailed off. There was no point in repeating what would only hurt Alan.

"I know what he said." Alan nodded. "But he must have changed his mind. There was a message from Vivian waiting for us when we got back to the hotel. I returned her call, and she told me to come right over to World Communications. Mr. Marshall wanted to congratulate me in person!"

"What made him change his mind?" Nancy could picture the sneer on George Marshall's lips as he mentioned Alan. She wouldn't have expected him to change his mind for all the gold in Fort Knox.

"I think it had something to do with Barton," Alan said.

"Barton!" Nancy sat straight up in her chair.

49

"'Yeah, that's the other piece of great news," Bess put in. "Alan saw him!"

"When? Where?" Nancy's head swam.

"Right after I went back to Marshall's office. Barton wanted to thank me for filling in for him, and he asked me to do his next couple of gigs while he stays out of the public eye for a while."

"You're kidding," Nancy said.

"Nope. He was hanging around, waiting for a limo to take him to his beach house, that purple bandanna around his neck, sitting in an armchair drinking a beer and watching some movie on a VCR." Alan leaned back in his chair with a happy sigh. "I guess he sort of coaxed Marshall into signing me on. And to think that until yesterday Barton was just someone I dreamed about meeting!"

"Nan, George, isn't it unbelievable?" Bess leaned over and grabbed Nancy's arm.

"Unbelievable," Nancy echoed, meaning it more literally than Bess had. Was she to believe that Harold Marshall had so completely changed his mind about Alan? Or that the only person Barton Novak had asked to see was not a member of his own band, not a close friend or relative, but a fan he'd spoken with for no more than a few minutes?

"Alan, are you *sure* about this?" she asked.

"Sure I'm sure." Alan grinned, his brown eyes shining. "Bess and I are going over to get a tour of the recording studios later this afternoon, and

Marshall's having Vivian draw the contracts up this week. So let's celebrate! Lunch is on me!"

The food was wonderful, and the weather at the outdoor patio was perfect, but throughout the rest of the meal, Nancy's thoughts spun. If Barton was fine, there was no mystery at all, was there? But what about the wallet and the two mysterious men? And what about Harold Marshall's offer to Alan? Just that morning, Marshall was calling Alan an idiot who "banged out a couple of Barton Novak's riffs." Now he was signing a record contract with him.

Nancy had an uncomfortable feeling in the pit of her stomach. Something was very wrong. But she kept her thoughts to herself until after Bess and Alan had left for World Communications. It wasn't until she and George were on their way back to the hotel that she confided her feelings.

"George, don't you think Alan's announcement was kind of, well, weird?"

"What do you mean, Nancy?"

"I mean, everything's happening so fast. One day Alan's taking guitar lessons in River Heights, and the next day he's signing a solo recording contract with one of the biggest labels in the business. George, we both know Alan's got a lot of talent, but this is just a little too much for me to believe."

"What's not to believe? By the end of the week, Alan's going to have a World Communications recording contract in his hands!" George was matter-of-fact. "I mean, it is pretty wild, but it's true."

"I don't know. What if Harold Marshall is stringing Alan along? I don't like that man."

"You think he might not come through?" George asked. "Then why would he make the offer in the first place?"

"I wish I could tell you." Nancy flung her hands up in despair. "I keep trying to get answers on this case, but all I get are more questions."

"And what about Barton?" George voiced one more of those questions as they rounded a corner and came to their hotel.

"Barton—a guy who agrees to disappear right before a concert he's spent months planning. It doesn't figure." Nancy pressed her lips together.

The doorman opened the hotel door, and Nancy and George crossed the tiled lobby floor to the front desk. "Well, what do you intend to do?" George asked.

The clerk on duty handed Nancy and George their keys and also gave Nancy a slip of paper with a telephone message on it. *Carl Rutland, security guard at Radio City Music Hall*, it said. *Found something you might want to know about.* A telephone number was written at the bottom.

"This might answer your question," Nancy told George. "Come on. Let's go up to my room and find out what Mr. Carl Rutland has to say."

* * *

As Nancy fitted her key in the lock, she heard her telephone ringing. "Maybe that's him calling back," she said to George. She pushed the door open and raced for the phone. "Hello?"

"Hi, beautiful," a male voice said.

"Ned! Hi!" Nancy felt herself smile at the sound of Ned Nickerson's mellow baritone. "How are you?"

"Curious, actually. I read in today's paper that Barton Novak vanished right before his concert, and I was wondering what happened. Weren't you supposed to hear Bent Fender play?"

Nancy eased herself onto the edge of the bed. "It's a pretty strange story. At first I was sure Barton had been kidnapped, but now it turns out that it's really just a publicity gimmick. I think. I mean, I don't know what to think. Ned, I don't know if I've got a mystery to solve or not." Nancy's words came out in a fast, nervous rush.

"Nan," Ned said slowly, "slow down and tell me all about it."

Nancy took a deep breath and recounted everything that had happened since her arrival in New York.

When she was done, Ned let out a long, low whistle. "Sounds like you've run into some people who play awfully rough. That blow on the head is serious. I don't like it at all," he said, worry rising with his voice.

"Ned, I'm fine," Nancy assured him. "The

53

worst part isn't the bump on my head. It's that I don't know if the wallet has anything to do with Barton or the two men backstage, or anything. I'm so keyed up. I don't know whether to forget this business or what."

"Well, how about a consultation?" Ned suggested. "Say, in about two hours? I can get on the road right away."

"You're coming up from school to spend some time with me in New York? Oh, Ned, that sounds great! I'm sure you can share Alan's room with him."

"Alan? You mean Bess's new superstar? The one who was offered the recording contract?"

Nancy frowned. "Yeah, Bess's superstar. And Ned, maybe you can help me figure out what's going on here."

"I'll do everything I can," Ned promised. "And if anyone tries to knock you over the head again, I'll give them a taste of their own medicine."

"My hero," Nancy giggled. "But don't forget, I'm the one with the brown belt in karate."

"Do you have to remind me?" Ned said, groaning.

"Well, I won't try any of my new moves on you this time," Nancy said solemnly. "Except maybe on the dance floor. Roger Gold is taking us to a wild new club tonight."

"Sounds great."

"Good. It's a date." Before saying goodbye,

Nancy gave Ned the address of the hotel. "There's an indoor parking lot right across the street," she added.

"Well, you look a little happier than you did a few minutes ago," George observed from the couch. "Love, love is the miracle drug," she sang teasingly. It was the refrain of one of Bent Fender's new songs.

"George, do you think Ned's ready to forget about Daryl?" Nancy felt herself blush.

"I don't know, Nan, but a few days together in the most exciting city in the world ought to do *something* for the two of you."

"Hmm. You know, this might turn out to be a good vacation after all. If I could just stop worrying about Barton, and Alan's record contract . . ." Nancy felt herself coming down to earth. "Speaking of which, I better call that security guard back."

She dialed the number on the message sheet. "Hello, is this Carl Rutland?" she asked the man who answered the telephone.

"Speaking."

"Hi, this is Nancy Drew. From the concert last night."

"Oh, Miss Drew. Yes. Hello."

"You said you found something?"

"That's right. Well, first of all, whoever gave you that knock on the head came in and out by the fire escape, off one of the dance studios. When I checked the windows leading out to it, I found that one of the latches had been forced open, and we always keep them locked."

"Mr. Rutland, do you think someone would go through all the trouble of climbing the fire escape and breaking in just to steal a wallet?" Nancy asked.

"Maybe. But it would be very risky. There are too many people around the Music Hall when there's a rock concert. You know, fans come without tickets and try to scalp them or just sneak in, and they wind up hanging around outside. Anyway, there'd be too good a chance of being caught."

"Then," Nancy mused aloud, "there must have been something worth far more than money in that wallet. Well, thank you for the information, Mr. Rutland."

"Wait, that's not the only thing I wanted to tell you," Carl Rutland said. "I found something outside Barton Novak's dressing room, near all those boxes and things."

"You did?" Nancy was alert.

"Yeah. A scarf. A violet-colored scarf with designs on it."

"Mr. Rutland," Nancy said hoarsely, in a flash of understanding, "you mean you found a purple bandanna—a square of heavy cotton, with a sort of leafy pattern stitched on it in green?"

"Yeah, that's it. Is it yours?"

"No. No, it's Barton Novak's, sort of his good luck charm," Nancy said, "and one of a kind.

His sister did the embroidery." Nancy remembered reading that in several articles about Barton. "He never plays a concert without it. Um, Mr. Rutland, when did you say you found the bandanna?"

"Last night, after they took you home. I've got it right here in my pocket."

"Last night?" Nancy's brain was working overtime. "Well, just hold on to it. I'll make arrangements to get it from you." Nancy thanked the man again and got off the phone in a hurry, her hand trembling as she hung up the receiver.

"Nancy, what's the matter? You look like that security guard has been telling you ghost stories or something," George said.

"No, not ghost stories. Something much more real and much more frightening. It's Alan, George. He's been lying to us!"

Chapter

Six

GEORGE'S EYES WIDENED. "What do you mean?"

"That guard found Barton's bandanna," Nancy explained.

"So? Maybe he dropped it without realizing."

"But don't you see?" Nancy felt sick at the realization. "Just this morning, Alan told us he saw Barton. And he said that Barton was wearing that bandanna!"

George began to look sick too. "Oh no."

"Even if he was a little flaky, I always thought I could trust Alan," Nancy said. "But now I don't know *what* he's gotten into—except that it's really dangerous." She got up and headed for the door.

"Hey, where are we going?" George grabbed a sweater from the bed.

"To find Alan." Nancy slipped on her jeans jacket and took the room key. "He and Bess must be getting their tour of the World recording studios right now." She put an insistent hand on George's back and moved her toward the door.

"Wouldn't it be easier to call him there?" George suggested.

Nancy shook her head vigorously. "No way. What if they wind up putting us through to Vivian or Mr. Marshall's office? I don't want them to know anything about this. I want to get Alan alone. Besides, I need to see the expression on his face when we confront him with his lie. It would be worth a thousand words, as they say." Nancy stepped out of the room.

George followed, a worried look in her brown eyes. "Nancy, do you think Bess knows Alan's lying? I mean, it seems so impossible—"

"I know. Bess has never been anything less than a hundred percent straight with us. I'm sure she wouldn't hold anything back. One thing really scares me, though. If Alan isn't the kind of guy we think he is, Bess could be in trouble." Nancy locked the room and headed for the elevator, with George a few steps behind her.

"But, Nancy, it's so obvious that the guy is

nuts about Bess. And don't forget, he helped us solve your last mystery."

"I know. I only hope he's got a good explanation for this."

Finding Alan turned out to be easier said than done. When Nancy and George arrived at World Communications, the receptionist told them that the recording facilities were not housed in the same building as the executive offices. "Our recording is done by an independent company. Oraye Sound." She wrote down Oraye's address.

"Is it far from here?" Nancy asked.

"All the way downtown."

Nancy took that to mean yes. "Come on, George. It looks like you and I are going for a little cab ride."

They raced outside and hailed a taxi. "205 East Fourth Street," Nancy told the driver. "And go whatever way's the fastest. It's important."

"Lady, it's always important. Everyone in this town is always in a hurry," the taxi driver responded. "But I'll do my best. Of course, going through midtown this time of day, there's always traffic."

"Isn't there some way to avoid it?" George asked. "This really is an emergency."

"Then you shoulda chartered a helicopter." The driver swung out into the flow of cars, inches in front of a gray hatchback. The driver of the gray car let out an angry blast of his horn.

"Oh brother," grumbled Nancy a few minutes later, looking nervously at her watch. "We could walk faster than this." She pulled several crinkled dollar bills out of her jacket pocket. "We'll get out here," she announced, before they had reached their destination. She pushed the money through the opening in the Plexiglas shield that separated the driver from his passengers. "Keep the change."

The taxi came to a halt, and she jumped out. "Come on, George. Maybe we can still make it down there before Bess and Alan leave."

The girls reached East Fourth Street in record time. "We should have recruited you for girls' track in high school," George panted.

Nancy wiped her forehead. "Let's see," she said, trying to catch her breath, "194, 196 . . . It must be on the other side of the street. 201. Yeah, there it is, 205."

Nancy rang the buzzer for Oraye Sound, Inc., and she and George entered the building and headed for the fifth floor. The elevator opened on a large area divided into a number of work spaces by movable partitions. Several halls branched off in different directions from the central space. People rushed back and forth busily, and the hum of voices filled the room. In one corner was a large desk that was not hidden behind any of the dividers; a young man sat behind it, typing.

Nancy and George approached him, and Nancy cleared her throat. He looked up from his typewriter. "Hi, are you with the NYU group?" he asked. "You're late," he continued, without waiting for an answer. "The tour's started already. They're down that way, in one of the editing rooms."

"NYU?" Nancy asked.

"Yes. New York University. Aren't you film students?"

Nancy shook her head. "Actually, we're here looking for our friends, Alan Wales and Bess Marvin."

"Who?"

"They should have come in early this afternoon. He's medium height with frizzy brown hair. She has blond hair a little past her shoulders, and she's on the short side," George supplied.

The man thought for a moment. "Oh, you mean the two Harold Marshall sent over."

Nancy's brow furrowed at Mr. Marshall's name. "Yes. That's right."

"Oh, you just missed them. They were talking about going out to celebrate something."

Nancy felt thoroughly frustrated as she and George started back across the large room. "George," she said, in what was for her a down voice. "What's going on with this case? I feel as if I'm following shadows, not leads." Now she wouldn't be able to get hold of Alan until their rendezvous at the club that evening. She'd lose several hours of sleuthing time—hours that could be critical to Barton Novak.

Before George could reply, Nancy saw something that made her pulse speed up. Moving as quickly as she could, she pulled George into an unoccupied work space. "It's Vivian!" she whispered, peeking out from around the partition.

"Who?"

"Harold Marshall's secretary." Nancy watched as Vivian emerged from the stairwell carrying a bulky package under her arm. The woman glanced around furtively and slipped down one of the hallways. The young man at the corner desk, his back to the work spaces and network of halls, continued to type, and Vivian passed by unnoticed.

"Looks to me like she's sneaking around," George said.

"Come on," Nancy urged. "Maybe the trip down here won't be a waste after all." She grabbed George's elbow, and silently, keeping a safe distance behind her, the girls followed Vivian down the hall.

Vivian seemed to know exactly where she was going. After proceeding along a maze of corridors past numerous doors, she stopped abruptly in front of one of them. Second-guessing the next move, Nancy pulled George back around the last corner in the corridor—and not a second too soon. Nancy edged around the corner just in time to see Vivian whipping her head around, clearly checking to make sure she was alone. Then she entered the room she had stopped in front of.

"Now what?" George hissed as they both breathed a sigh of relief.

"Well, we can't follow her in there," Nancy thought out loud, "so we'll have to wait until she leaves. Then we can see what's in that room. But let's get out of here. She's going to come back this way, and besides, someone might see us."

"Maybe there's a ladies' room around here," George suggested. "We could hide in there until she leaves."

The girls found one a few doors down and entered cautiously, making sure it was unoccupied. Then Nancy posted herself by the door, leaving it open a finger's width so she could peer out.

Vivian didn't take long. Only a few minutes later, Nancy heard the clicking of her high-heeled black pumps on the tiled hallway floor and noticed that Vivian no longer carried the package that had been under her arm. "She must have dropped something off," Nancy said, pulling the restroom door shut as Vivian walked by.

Nancy waited until the footsteps faded. Then she peeked out again. The corridor was empty.

"Okay, *now!*" she instructed George. The two friends made a dash for the room Vivian had entered and let themselves inside, the door opening and closing with a faint squeak.

The walls of the small room were lined, floor to ceiling, with cabinets, and in the middle of the room were low, free-standing, enclosed bins.

"It's some kind of storeroom," Nancy observed.

She pulled at the handle of one of the cabinets —labeled 1981, A through C—and found it locked. She tried one on the adjacent wall. The typed sticker on the door read 1982, G through K. It didn't open either.

George was walking around, fiddling with the cabinet doors. "These are locked too," she said, her words colored with annoyance. Then she called out softly, "Nancy, come look at this."

When Nancy joined her, the young detective took a look at a list George had been studying. It was taped to the wall. The page was divided into columns headed *name, title of master, date borrowed, date returned.*

"Masters. So that's why all these drawers are locked so securely. George, this is where they keep all the original recordings, the ones they copy when they press the albums they sell."

"Right," George said, "I remember back when we were sophomores, this record store in Mount Harmon was closed down because the owner was selling albums that had been made illegally. I'm not sure of the details, but he was buying the albums for way under the normal costs, selling them for the retail prices, and raking in a fortune."

Nancy nodded. "Right. If these masters get into the wrong hands, they can be used to make a lot of illegal money. Record piracy, I think they call it."

As Nancy talked, she skimmed the list in front of her for Vivian's name. It wasn't there. *What was Vivian up to?* she wondered. She guessed that the parcel contained masters Vivian had sneaked out and then sneaked back in. Was Vivian getting them for Harold Marshall so he could mint illegal albums and sell them as the real thing? If so, then Barton was right to wonder about Bent Fender's royalties. They wouldn't earn money on copies sold illegally.

Nancy pondered that, continuing to study the list. Suddenly a familiar name near the bottom of the page caught her eye. "George!" she gasped, pointing to the bold script.

George's gaze followed Nancy's finger. "Oh wow! Barton Novak!"

"And he was here just a few days ago!" Nancy added. "George, I bet Barton came here and discovered something. Maybe he found out that some of the masters were missing!"

"And then someone found out that Barton

knew, and had to make sure he didn't tell anyone."

Nancy nodded, her face taut. "That's a really strong motive. Now I'm sure Barton didn't disappear on his own. He must have been kidnapped!"

Chapter

Seven

THE PIECES OF the puzzle were finally beginning to fall into place. "This explains why there was no ransom note," Nancy continued. "Barton's kidnappers weren't interested in getting money, just in keeping him from spilling the beans. I bet all this has something to do with his wanting to talk to me after the concert." Nancy leaned back against one of the cabinets, digesting the implications of the new discovery.

Suddenly, a thought occurred to her that made her blood go colder than an arctic ice floe. "George," she said, "if Barton's kidnappers don't want a ransom for him, maybe they don't intend to free him at all."

George's ruddy complexion drained to pale.

The two girls stood in silence, the horrible realization sinking in until the stillness in the room was shattered by the soft but unmistakable squeal of the door opening. Nancy gasped.

A sandy-haired man with a mustache stepped inside. There was no place to escape his gaze in the small room. "Who are you?" he asked gruffly. "No unauthorized personnel allowed in here."

Nancy thought quickly. "We, um . . . we're with the NYU group."

"Film students," George added, backing up Nancy's story.

"Oh. Well, what are you kids doing in here? Your group is over in one of the editing rooms." He motioned for them to leave. "Down this hall and to the left."

For a moment, Nancy was flooded with a sense of relief. "Oh. Thank you, sir." She and George moved toward the door.

But as soon as they were safely out of Oraye Sound and outside again, Nancy's relief dissolved in a flood of nerves. What if she couldn't locate Barton before it was too late? Or was it already too late? Who was at the bottom of the sordid mess, and how much did Alan know about it? How safe was Bess if she inadvertently had been caught smack in the middle of a record pirating conspiracy?

Stop! Nancy admonished herself. Standing in the middle of a busy New York street thinking about all this wasn't going to get her any closer to answering the questions that were gnawing at her. She took several breaths, taking the air deep into her body and breathing from her stomach, the way she'd been taught in karate class.

"Okay," she told George, "the first thing to do is to find out which people have access to the room with the masters in it, and then find out what they know." Nancy made a beeline for the nearest pay phone, fishing around in her jeans pocket as she ran.

A loud, jarring crackle came out of the earpiece as she picked up the receiver. "Broken." She slammed down the phone and moved over to the next one. "Good," she told George. "This one's got a dial tone." She pulled her little notebook out of her shoulder bag and quickly turned the pages until she found Roger Gold's number.

Be home. Please be home. She punched out his number on the pushbutton telephone.

"Hello?" Roger's voice came over the wire.

"Roger. It's Nancy Drew. Thank goodness you're there."

"Nancy, what's wrong? Is it about Barton? Do you know where he is?"

"Not yet," Nancy replied, trying to keep from sounding frightened, "but I think I've got my first solid lead."

"Was he kidnapped?" Roger sounded nervous.

"Yes, I think so."

"I knew it! No way did Barton go off on his own. He was too involved in those concerts." Roger paused. "So what do you think's going on?"

"I think someone's pirating Bent Fender's records. And probably other groups' records, too."

"Pirating our records?" A string of angry words streamed out of Roger Gold's normally soft-speaking mouth. Nancy waited for him to calm down. "I'm sorry," he said finally. "Listening to me get mad isn't going to help Barton, is it?"

"That's okay, Roger. I'm not exactly a bearer of good tidings. But there is something you can tell me that will help get to the bottom of this."

"Anything."

"Who has access to the cabinets in the masters room at Oraye Sound?"

"Well, all the techies—the recording technicians—at Oraye, for starters. And they usually give a key to the musicians who record there."

"Like you and Barton and the rest of the band?"

"Right. I mean, we do most of our work at our own private studios, but we do some mixing and stuff there sometimes. Yeah."

"Anyone else?" Nancy asked.

"The top executives at World," Roger said.

"Harold Marshall?"

A moment of silence, then Roger exploded. "Is that creep in on Barton's disappearance?"

"Well, he has an interesting reason for why Barton didn't make the concert."

"I don't buy it," Roger said firmly, after hearing Harold Marshall's story. "Barton would want the sales of our records to center around our music, not around gossip about where he is. Besides, he doesn't like the idea of people poking around in his private life. Nope. Marshall's story just doesn't make sense."

Nancy wasn't surprised by Roger's opinion. Marshall's story had too many holes in it for her to swallow it completely. "Roger, thank you. You've been a big help. Oh, and one more thing. How does Harold Marshall get along with his secretary?"

"Vivian? They're a perfect team. The witch and the warlock. Marshall thinks she's the greatest thing since stereophonic sound. The rat has had his eye on her since the day she came to work for him. And she'll do anything he asks. And I mean anything."

"Roger, would Vivian do Marshall's dirty work?" Nancy pictured Vivian sneaking into the masters room.

"Sure."

"And would Marshall be low enough to pirate his own company's records and pocket the profit?"

"That toad is low enough to do anything," Roger answered.

"You know, it's possible that we might have our man," Nancy said. "But we have to catch him in the act to make sure."

"You just tell me what I have to do to help," Roger offered. "I'd be only too happy to nail that bum."

"The best thing you can do is act as if nothing's happened. Meet us at the club tonight, work on your new songs, do whatever you would normally do. We don't want Marshall to think we're on to him." Nancy inhaled sharply. "Because if Barton's disappearance is any indication, what we know could be hazardous to our health!"

She hung up the phone and looked at George. "Come on. We've got to find out a lot more before we crack this case."

"Action!" George rubbed her hands together. "This is the part I like the best."

Nancy shook her head. "I'm not so sure this is action you'll enjoy . . ."

"Ugh. I feel like I'm back in school again," George moaned.

"School was never a life-or-death situation," Nancy responded gravely. "Now read."

The girls were seated in the research room of the Jefferson Market Library, a brisk walk from the studios of Oraye Sound. Books and back copies of magazines were piled next to them on the old wooden tables.

Nancy skimmed through an article in *Allegro*, the monthly newspaper of the musicians' union. "George, listen to this." She read out loud, keeping her voice low, so as not to disturb the people around her. " 'One billion dollars per year are lost in residuals, due to pirated sound and video recordings in the United States and abroad.' One billion dollars worth of royalty money! Can you believe that?" she exclaimed. "Wow, I had no idea what a huge black market there is for pirated recordings. There's certainly enough money at stake to make some crook want to get rid of anyone in the way."

Nancy's stomach did a slow somersault as she thought about Barton's safety.

"Nancy, here's something," George whispered a moment later. "Certain countries have no copyright laws at all. They simply obtain existing printed or recorded materials from other countries and publish or manufacture copies of their own, or they purchase pirated copies at a cost far below the market value. No revenue from these sales goes to the artist or company that holds the copyright."

Nancy listened intently. "Wow! You mean somebody could take records that were made illegally here and sell them in certain other places where there are no copyright laws?"

"Right."

"And these foreign governments wouldn't consider it a crime?"

George nodded and continued, her brown-eyed gaze gliding across the page as she read. "The one major country to operate without copyright laws is the People's Republic of China."

"China!" A bell went off in Nancy's head. "George, that wallet I found backstage during the concert—it had a dragon on it—a Chinese dragon! I wonder if that's more than just a coincidence." Nancy rested her elbow on the table and propped her chin on the palm of her hand.

"Do you think Harold Marshall might have some connection to the Chinese?" George asked. "Or Vivian? Somehow, I can't imagine her trudging through rice paddies in those high-heeled shoes." George let out a giggle, despite the severity of the situation. Then she clapped a hand over her mouth. "Sorry, Nan."

But Nancy wasn't at all annoyed with George. "You're a genius!" she said excitedly, trying at the same time to keep her voice down. "Maybe Vivian wouldn't be able to wing it on a tour of the rice fields, but I know someone who would."

"Nancy, what are you talking about?"

"That picture you had of Vivian reminded me of a poster I saw of Chinese workers harvesting rice. I saw it just this morning . . . hanging on the wall in Ann Nordquist's office!" Nancy grabbed George's arm. "Ann is Bent Fender's agent. And she just came back from China. She was telling my dad and me about her trip." Nancy's pulse was racing. "What if that wallet belongs to her? And what if she wasn't just sight-seeing?"

"But what about Mr. Marshall?" George reminded her.

"Yes, then there's Harold Marshall." Nancy pondered that for a few moments. "You know, he and Ann Nordquist both made a point of telling me how much they disliked each other. But what if they did that just to throw me off the track? It's possible they're working together."

"But Nancy, you told me that Ann Nordquist seemed like a nice woman."

"She did. I mean, she does. I liked her. And I don't see why she would own a wallet with the initial L. Still, I don't think we can rule her out entirely. You can never be too sure."

"I guess not. We thought Alan was playing straight with us, and look what happened. If he drags Bess into this, he's going to be really sorry."

Nancy nodded. "Speaking of which, let's get back to the hotel. I want to pick up Ned and get to the club. Bess's wonder boy and I are in for a little heart-to-heart." She gathered up the books and bound volumes of magazines and began replacing them on the shelves. "And," she added, "I think I ought to do a little checking up on Ms. Ann Nordquist."

"Yeah," George said. "Maybe she got tired of earning her ten percent and decided to make a real killing."

"I hope it hasn't gone that far." Nancy hesitated before going on. ". . . As far as murder."

Chapter

Eight

NED!" NANCY THREW her arms around the tall, broad-shouldered young man. "Sorry to keep you waiting. Have you been here long?" Nancy had found Ned sitting on the plush velvet sofa in the hotel lobby.

"Got here just about five minutes ago," Ned said, bending down to give her a powerful hug. A lock of thick dark hair fell forward over his eye, and Nancy brushed it away.

"I want you to know," she said, her mind still reeling from her frenzied afternoon, "your visit is the one bright spot in this entire trip."

"Uh-oh. Sounds like my favorite detective is

wrapped up in a tough case. What's happened since we talked on the phone?"

Nancy let out a sigh. "First I had so few real clues that I didn't even know if I had a mystery or not. Now, all of a sudden, there are all sorts of leads . . . and I don't know which ones to follow first." Nancy could see George coming across the lobby with the room keys she had picked up from the front desk. "Listen, why don't you come upstairs, and I'll tell you everything?"

A few minutes later, the three friends were seated around the table in the main room of the suite, drinking the Cokes they had ordered from room service. Nancy and George recounted the day's events, from the newspaper headlines about Barton to their library research.

Ned looked thoughtful. "So you think the trail of evidence could lead to that record producer—"

"Harold Marshall," George supplied.

"Right, or the Nordquist woman, or even Alan?" Ned's voice dropped as he uttered Bess's boyfriend's name. "So, I'm sharing a room with one of your suspects, Nancy?"

Nancy shrugged. "I haven't even seen Alan since you called, so I haven't had a chance to ask him about sharing his room. And once I confront him about his lie, I'm not sure how generous he's going to feel about doing any favors for my friends." Nancy twisted a strand of hair around her index finger. "But don't worry. There's a couch in Dad's room. I'm sure he wouldn't mind having you stay with us."

As if on cue, the door to the suite opened, and Carson Drew stepped inside. "Ned! Well, hello. I thought I heard your voice. It's good to see you again."

Ned stood up, and they shook hands. "Good to be here, Mr. Drew."

"So." Carson Drew turned toward his daughter and George. "Anything new on the case?"

"As a matter of fact, Dad, yes. I was wondering if you could arrange another meeting between me and Ann Nordquist. I need to talk to her."

"I'm sure she'd be happy to. In fact, I'll ask her tonight at dinner."

"You mean you're having another business meeting?" Nancy wondered if she should tell her father that Ann Nordquist was on her list of suspects. No, she decided. She'd keep it to herself until she had more information.

Carson Drew liked to tease his daughter, to remind her that her detective's methods were a direct contrast to his own lawyer's procedure.

"Not exactly," he replied. "Actually, I asked her to dine with me more for pleasure."

Nancy felt a chill race through her. "For pleasure?" she echoed dully. Normally she would have been happy that her father had a dinner date. Her mother had died when she was a very little girl, and she felt it had been too long that her father had done without female companionship. He dated occasionally, but for the most part, when he had free time, he threw himself into extra work projects. But Ann Nordquist? The woman had seemed nice, but Nancy couldn't get the China connection out of her mind.

"Yes, for pleasure." Carson Drew chuckled. "Your old father deserves to enjoy himself occasionally. And I find Ann Nordquist a very attractive, highly intelligent woman."

Nancy swallowed hard. "Oh," she said, exchanging looks with George and Ned. "Well, I—I hope you have fun." Her voice came out in a high, tight squeak. What if her father were going out with one of Barton Novak's kidnappers?

"Psycho killer . . ." Vintage rock blared from the speakers, and dancers spun beneath the ultraviolet lights. The club was a study in downtown funk. A stage had been set up at the front, and the people milling around in the crowded room ranged from the utmost in fashionable to the totally outrageous.

"Wow! Check *that* get-up," Ned said, tapping Nancy on the arm.

A girl with a rainbow-colored bristle of hair walked by the table where they sat, her slender body draped in black satin and lace.

"What? Oh, yeah, I see her," Nancy replied distractedly, glancing at the girl for only a brief second. Quickly, she turned her attention back to the entrance of the club, which was visible from her balcony perch. The second Alan and Bess walked through that doorway, she wanted to know about it.

"Nan, they'll be here soon," Ned assured her gently. "Meanwhile, you might as well enjoy yourself. How often do you get to come to a place like this?" He reached out and trailed his fingers up her back.

Nancy could feel the electric tingle of his touch. She inched her chair closer to his and rested her head on his shoulder, the softness of his sweater caressing her cheek. "Oh, Ned, I'm sorry. I guess I'm not a very good date."

"You're the best. I just wish I could do something to cheer you up."

"Ned, sometimes I don't think I deserve you. You come all the way from school to be with me, and I'm so wrapped up in this case I'm no fun at all."

"Hey, it's okay. This is me, remember? I've stuck by you during lots of tough cases. I know what you're going through."

Nancy lifted her head and looked into Ned's brown eyes, her gaze holding his. "You're not mad at me, are you, about what happened on the last case?"

She couldn't quite bring herself to pronounce Daryl's name. Sure, she'd been a willing victim of Daryl's sexy eyes and smooth personality, but it had been Ned who'd bailed her out of a dangerous situation during that case, and Ned who had been there for her once the criminals were safely behind bars.

Ned cupped her face in his large hands. "It hurt, sure. I mean, if it hadn't, I'd have to start wondering how much I really love you. And Nancy, I do love you."

Nancy held her breath, afraid to break the spell of the moment. But when Ned's tender gaze left her face, she followed his glance.

"Alan!" She was on her feet, the tough detective back in top form. "Let's go!"

Nancy and Ned flew down the back staircase and caught up with Alan and Bess at the coat checkroom. The attendant was already hanging up George's coat. She must have gone ahead to check out the dance floor.

"Nan! Hi. And Ned!" Bess gave him an exuberant hug while Alan greeted Nancy easily. "Hi. How're you doing?"

Nancy steeled herself. "I'd be a lot better if I could figure out why you lied to me about seeing Barton Novak."

Bess spun around, looking like she'd just been slapped. "What do you mean?" Her voice rose. "Alan wouldn't lie, would you?" she asked, moving quickly to his side.

Alan looked from Nancy to Bess, and then back to Nancy. "I, ah—"

Bess was gazing up at Alan, who met her eyes

and held her glance for a moment that seemed to go on forever. Nancy watched nervously. She couldn't imagine anything worse than getting caught between them.

"No," Alan said finally, his voice stronger, "of course I wouldn't lie."

"You told me you saw Barton wearing his purple bandanna," Nancy said accusingly.

"That's right."

"Alan, the security guard at Radio City Music Hall found Barton's bandanna last night after we left. He's had it ever since."

Alan's cheeks blazed under the colored lights. "Well, maybe . . . maybe there are two bandannas."

Nancy felt a rush of annoyance. Why was Alan playing games with her? "You know as well as I do that it's a one-of-a-kind good luck charm. Every article written about Barton mentions that."

Alan shifted from one foot to the other. Bess's gaze was still frozen on him. "So, um, suppose I remembered wrong. Suppose he wasn't wearing the bandanna. What's the big deal?" He raised his eyes and looked at Bess, a note of pleading in his voice. "You believe I saw him, don't you?"

"Of course I do," Bess responded. She whirled to face Nancy. "What's gotten into you?" she snapped.

Bess's angry tone stung Nancy like a bitter

wind. "Bess, I don't mean to hurt you, but I don't think Alan is telling the truth. Doesn't it strike you as a little weird that in the last two days, one of the few people to have any contact with Barton Novak is someone who barely knows him? Not even Barton's sister or his best friends have heard from him."

"Why would I lie?" Alan said after what felt like an interminable pause. "I feel kind of like Barton's my brother. I mean, I learned all about rock and roll from listening to him. Now we're even recording on the same label."

"That's just it! Frankly, Alan, your instant success hasn't felt right to me since the second you told me. We all know how good you are, but you're not a professional. Not yet. And World is a label for professionals. You know what I think? I think Harold Marshall offered you that contract in return for throwing me off the scent."

Nancy waited for Alan's response, but it was Bess who jumped forward, her face inches from Nancy's, her hands clenched. *"Nancy Drew!* I thought you were one of my very best friends. What a jerk I was. Alan got that contract on talent. Pure talent. And if you're too dense to realize that, at least you ought to keep your opinions to yourself!" She spun on her heels, grabbing Alan's arm and maneuvering him away. "We don't need to waste our time with people like that," Nancy heard her say.

"Wait, Bess!" Nancy called out frantically. She started after her friend, but Ned put out a restraining hand.

"Nancy, why don't you wait until she's cooled off."

"She's never going to cool off, Ned. Bess is going to hate me forever." Nancy watched her friend storm off, rigid with fury, never once looking back.

Chapter

Nine

GEORGE WHIRLED AROUND the dance floor with one partner after another—first Linda Ferrare's cousin, then Jim Parker, and finally a friend Jim had brought with him. Across the room, Bess was also dancing, laughing and clearly making a show of having a wonderful time.

But Nancy's feet seemed to stick to the floor. Her body barely swayed to the song pulsing in the smoky air.

"Nancy, maybe we ought to call it a night," Ned shouted over the loud music.

Nodding her head wearily, Nancy stopped dancing. Ned put his arm around her shoulders and guided her off the floor. "I'll bet Bess doesn't stay mad at you for more than a few hours," he consoled her.

Nancy's glance strayed to Bess and Alan, who were rocking to an old Rolling Stones tune. As if sensing that she was being watched, Bess turned and shot icy daggers with her glance across the crowded room. Then she guided Alan around, leaving Nancy to stare at her back. "I don't know," Nancy said glumly. "Besides, it's not just Bess. It's Barton and the record pirating and my father going out with Ann Nordquist . . ."

"Look, at this point, you don't know if Ann Nordquist is anything more than an enthusiastic tourist, right?" Ned asked. "She might not have anything to do with the pirating at all."

"Maybe not. I mean, she did seem really sweet when I met her, but the Chinese connection is the only plausible link I've been able to turn up so far between that wallet I found and the record scam."

"The key words are 'so far,' Nan. You don't know anything for certain yet. So how about if we head back to the hotel and you try to relax and get a good night's rest. Tomorrow you'll have lots of energy. Maybe you'll be able to crack this case once and for all."

The corners of Nancy's mouth turned up for the first time all evening. "Okay, Mom."

"Just giving you good, sensible advice, my dear," teased Ned in a high voice.

They got their coats and said their goodbyes,

making plans to have breakfast with George the next morning.

"See you in the hotel dining room," George said as Nancy and Ned were leaving. "And Nancy, don't get freaked out about Bess. She'll come around. She loves you to pieces, just like I do."

Nancy gave George a big hug. "Thanks. You're the best."

"Yeah, you're a good friend," Ned agreed, giving George an affectionate pat on the back.

"Hey, hey, please. You don't want me to get a swollen ego, do you?" George winked.

Nancy and Ned headed for the exit. Cool, crisp air greeted Nancy as she stepped outside. She inhaled the night, savoring the relative quiet after the pulsing music and din of voices in the club. The street was dark. Except for a street-lamp down the block, the only source of light was the club's marquee.

"Something catch your eye?" Ned asked.

"No. Just thinking what this street must look like in the daytime. Pretty dingy, I guess." Nancy's eyes slowly gazed up and down the street.

"Yeah, there's some difference between the junk piled out here and the way the club's fixed up." Ned's hand gently took hold of Nancy's. "Do you want to walk for a while? It may be seedy down here, but I don't think it's dangerous."

Nancy smiled. Maybe now was a good time for

them to work on their relationship. "I'd love a walk with you, Ned. Dangerous or not."

Ned could feel the sincerity in her words. Slowly he leaned forward to kiss her.

"Ned? Ned Nickerson?" The mood was broken by a short young man who was leaving the club behind them. He rushed up to them, brushing his wavy brown hair out of one eye.

Ned took a hard look at him. "Dave, isn't it?"

"Yeah. Dave Peck. Long time no see, buddy." Dave stuck out a leather-gloved hand, and Nancy could see a thick gold chain bracelet studded with gems that sparkled under the streetlights.

Ned grasped Dave's hand in his. "Yes . . . a long time. I guess I didn't recognize you all . . . all dressed up."

"Yup. Great new threads, don't you think?" Dave patted his leather jacket, which was decorated with tucks and folds and numerous zippers. He wore it open, revealing a short, muscular body in a pair of beige slacks and a silk shirt, several of the top buttons open to show off more gold jewelry. On his feet were a pair of green snakeskin cowboy boots.

"Oh, Nancy, this is Dave Peck. We know each other from school. Dave, my girlfriend, Nancy."

"Hello," Nancy said, trying to imagine Dave at Emerson College. Somehow she couldn't quite picture him burning the midnight oil. At least not over books.

As Dave turned toward her, the smile on his

face slipped away. He stared at her with his mouth open, his eyes wide, as if she were a frightening vision from the past.

"Is something wrong?" Nancy asked.

Dave gave his head a hard shake. "Oh . . . no. No, I'm happy to meet you." He grasped her hand, and through his tight gloves Nancy could feel a large ring on one finger. "Any pal of Nickerson's is a pal of mine." He turned his attention back to Ned. "So, what's happening?"

"The usual," Ned responded politely. "Studying, going to classes. Midterms are coming up in a few weeks."

"So, you're just in town for a vacation?"

Ned nodded. "We had Friday off because Emerson is hosting an education conference. I decided to spend the three-day weekend here with Nancy. How about you? What are you doing these days?"

Clearly that was the question Dave had been waiting for. "Man, I've got to tell you, dropping out of school was the best thing I ever did."

So that's his story, Nancy thought.

"Life is great," Dave went on. "Couldn't be better. No more forcing myself to get up in the morning and go to classes. No more tests or papers. I do what I want. Lots of money, lots of chicks." He gave a lewd laugh and flashed Ned a thumbs-up sign. "No offense to the little lady," he added to Nancy.

Nancy gritted her teeth.

"Yup. This is a great town if you're into success. Got myself a great little business."

"You've got your own business?" Ned blurted out.

"Well, actually I've got a—sort of a partner," Dave hedged.

Nancy found herself betting anything that Dave's so-called partner was, in truth, his boss. She could tell that Ned didn't quite buy his story either. Though whatever Dave was doing, it was plain that he did have money to throw around.

"So, what is it you do?" Ned asked, as if reading Nancy's mind. "I wouldn't mind a little extra pocket money," he kidded.

"A little of this, a little of that," Dave replied vaguely. "But I still like to keep up with the rock scene. No better place for it in the world than right here in this city."

"I guess not," Ned said. "Well, it was nice talking to you, Dave. We'd better get going."

"Sure. There's my limo anyhow." Dave pointed to a black stretch limo pulling around the corner and stopping across the street from the club.

"Wow, that's some car." Ned couldn't hide his astonishment.

"She's a beaut, huh?" Dave said smugly. "Well, good bumping into you, pal. Nice to meet you, Nancy." His words were cordial, but Nancy caught the peculiar look in his eye again as he addressed her.

" 'Bye, Dave." Nancy watched him go, stepping into the street. She gave a little shudder. Dave was definitely not her idea of a nice guy. And she seemed to make him uncomfortable, too.

"What is it about him?" she said to Ned. "He gives me the creeps."

"Yeah, he's pretty weird. Truth is, he didn't drop out of school; he got kicked out. Never did a bit of work. I don't know why he was there in the first place. The only thing he seemed at all into was his part-time job at the Emerson Record World. But there was some problem there too. I have the feeling he got fired. Anyway, I stopped seeing him there when I went in to buy albums. Pretty soon after that, I stopped seeing him around campus at all."

"A record store, Ned?" Nancy asked, a funny feeling in the pit of her stomach. "Isn't it a little weird, all this record stuff?" Nancy watched Dave climb into the back of the limo. Then the thought hit like a cyclone. "Oh no, Ned!" Her voice was low. "He fits the exact description."

"What description? What are you saying?"

"I think Dave might have been one of the guys backstage the night Barton disappeared! He could even have been the one who hit me over the head. Maybe that's why he kept giving me such funny looks!"

Nancy darted from the club entrance into the

street, determined to make out the license plate before the limo vanished. But just as she passed a pile of crates, Ned cried, "Nancy, look out!" Nancy had never heard such panic in his voice. She turned suddenly, looking back at him, but lost her balance.

As she fell, her eyes caught the glint of something metallic cutting through the air and heading straight for her. Her body slammed onto the sidewalk as a knife jammed into a crate just inches away. It quivered there, giving its serpentine handle the illusion of movement.

Ned was by her side in seconds, but Nancy was already on her feet, running down the street as the limo pulled around a corner. "It stopped for a moment," she said, "as if they were waiting to see what would happen."

The limo was too far ahead to catch, but she did see the license plate. The numbers were caked with mud, but the decoration on the right side was clearly visible: a dragon with its tail curved into an L! Then it turned the corner and sped off into the night.

"Did you see the dragon?" Nancy asked breathlessly.

"Yeah, I saw it. Nancy, are you all right?"

"I guess so." She trembled at the thought of her near brush with death. "The fall didn't hurt much, but that knife came pretty close. Come on, let's get it. Someone has finally given us our first real clue!"

Cautiously they ran to the pile of crates where Nancy had fallen. "The police might be able to lift some—" She came to a sudden stop and stared in amazement at the crate. "It's gone! The knife is *gone!*"

Chapter

Ten

THEN WE FLAGGED a cab and tried to follow him, but he was too far ahead of us. We couldn't find him," Nancy told George, spearing a french fry and popping it into her mouth.

"So first thing this morning we called the manager of the Emerson Record World." Ned picked up where Nancy had left off. "It turns out that Dave Peck was fired for buying cheap pirated records. He charged the store the regular price, then deposited the extra money in his personal account! They got wise to what he was doing when one of the stockroom clerks discovered that the codes on the records were missing."

"You're kidding!" George put down her coffee

cup with a chink. "Wow! That sleazy guy could play a really important part in this mystery, huh?"

"You know it." Nancy finally felt she was on the trail that would crack this case. "I bet anything Dave's ring has a dragon on it," she went on, "and his ring and license plate match the wallet I found at the Music Hall. If the wallet belongs to Dave, maybe Ann Nordquist is in the clear."

"A good thing, since she and your dad are spending the day together," Ned remarked. "I think he really likes her."

"Hmm, I can't say I'm entirely comfortable with that," Nancy admitted. "And I won't be until I know what's going on."

George nodded. "Well, one way or the other, the truth will come out, as they say. So, anyhow, what'd you do next?"

"Well, the record store didn't know where to get in touch with him, so Ned called up the Emerson College registrar's office. His roommate works there a few hours a day, and Ned talked him into looking up Dave's mother's telephone number. The problem is she doesn't answer. We're going to try her again after breakfast."

George nodded. "Well, if there's anything I can do . . ."

"Thanks. I'll definitely let you know," Nancy said. "So, now that we've told you about the rest of our night, how was yours?"

"Pretty good. They played some really hot dancing music. But we didn't stay all that long after you guys left. Everyone was kind of keyed up about Barton. Roger especially."

"I can understand that," Nancy said. "What are he and the rest of the band going to do about tonight's performance if Barton's still a no show by concert time?"

"Alan," George said simply.

Nancy groaned. "I was afraid of that. You know, if Alan keeps getting to fill in on these gigs, he's never going to come clean with what he knows about Barton. I mean, why should he? As long as Barton's not around, Alan's a star."

"And is he playing the part," George added. "He took Bess over to the Hard Rock Cafe for a midnight supper after we left the club. He said all the biggest names in the music world hang out there. I think he was counting himself as one of them."

Nancy's expression grew dark. "I can't believe Bess. She's buying in to Alan's fantasy without stopping to consider how much harm he might be doing."

"So you really think Alan's hiding something? I mean, I know he's on another planet these days, but do you really think he'd put Barton's life in danger?"

"The only way to answer that question is to get to the bottom of whatever's going on," Nancy said. "Speaking of which, we'd better start calling Dave's mother again." She finished up her eggs and pushed her plate away. "Ready?" She stood up.

"Reporting for duty, Detective Drew," Ned replied, and the three friends stood up.

Several hours later, in the Drews' suite, they still were having no luck. Ned dialed Mrs. Peck's number for what seemed to Nancy like the thousandth time, and Nancy and George held their breath. "One ring," Ned announced. "Two. Three."

Nancy rolled her eyes in frustration.

"Hello? Is this Mrs. Peck?"

Ned began talking, and Nancy sat up straight and hung on to his every word.

"Mrs. Peck, my name is Ned Nickerson. I'm a—a friend of Dave's," Ned fibbed, looking slightly sheepish.

"We went to school together, Mrs. Peck," Ned went on. "Yes, as a matter of fact, I saw him just last night." Ned seemed relieved to be saying something truthful. "But he forgot to give me his address. That's why I'm calling, actually." Ned paused, his brow furrowed. "You don't?" He rolled his eyes. "If you'll excuse my saying so, that's—well, that's a little surprising to me."

"George," Nancy exclaimed. "How can a man's own mother not have his address? There is definitely something weird going on."

"Yes, I see," Ned said, signaling for quiet. "Then, do you know who his partner is? Oh, his boss—okay. His name is Lee? But you don't know how to contact him either?" Nancy's heart sank.

"Whew!" Ned sighed when he finally hung up the phone. "If I hadn't said I had to go, she would have gone on all day."

"So tell," Nancy demanded, a touch impatiently.

"Oh, sorry, Nan. Well, Dave's mother obviously thinks Dave's the greatest thing since sliced bread, even though she's disappointed he left school."

"But she doesn't know where he is half the time," Nancy put in.

"She told me his work takes him to so many places he can't have a permanent address. But she sure was quick to add that he calls her every week."

"To keep up the image of the perfect son," George observed.

"Except that he lives out of a suitcase," Nancy said. "All set to pick up and move if anyone's on his tail."

Ned agreed. "That business Dave's involved in can't be aboveboard. Anyway, his mother said his boss is a guy named Lee. James Lee. She started telling me how this Lee took her and 'her Davey' out to some restaurant in New York that Lee's brother owns. She would have told me what they had eaten, too, if I'd let her." He shook his head. "You know, I felt bad misleading her about Dave and me. She seemed kind of lonely."

"Poor woman. She probably deserves a lot better than Dave," Nancy said sympathetically. "When I get my hands on him . . ."

"But Nan, he doesn't have an address," George reminded her friend. "How are you going to find him?"

Nancy was silent for several minutes, contemplating. "Listen, Dave said he likes to keep up with the music scene, right?"

"Right," Ned affirmed.

"Well, isn't tonight's concert the most talked about show around? Bent Fender plays 'Rock for Relief' at the Rotunda," Nancy said, paraphrasing a radio advertisement, "the chic nightspot everyone wants to be seen at."

"Yeah, Roger was telling us last night that there will be huge crowds of people outside the Rotunda begging the doormen to let them pay their twenty-dollar admission charge and come inside," George injected. "Doesn't that sound nuts?"

"When you're hot, you're hot," Ned said, grinning. "But I see what you're getting at, Nancy. This is just the kind of scene a guy like Dave wouldn't miss."

"Exactly. So all we have to do is show up—and keep our fingers crossed that Dave will too."

* * *

"Wow! Look at all those people," Nancy exclaimed as she, Ned, and George arrived at the Rotunda later that evening. "How're they all going to fit inside?"

"A lot of them aren't," Ned replied. "That's part of the gimmick. If you keep a huge crowd of people standing outside your club, dying to get in, everyone will think it's popular, the place to be. And everyone who gets in will feel extra special about being there—you know, a member of the elite."

"Yuck. I'd have too much pride to stand out here praying the doormen would pick me out of the crowd." George wrinkled her nose in disgust.

"I'm with you," agreed Nancy. "It's a good thing we're on the guest list." They walked around to a lane cordoned off for guests of the club and people with free passes.

"You're on my list too," Ned whispered in Nancy's ear, his lips grazing her cheek.

Nancy almost melted. "And you're on mine," she said. Ned looked so handsome in his jeans and black pullover sweater. But despite her confident manner, Nancy still wondered about their relationship. The two of them needed time to relax together, time to really laugh and let loose and put their problems in the past, where they belonged. Until the mystery was solved, that would be impossible.

Once they were inside the club, Nancy's thoughts turned to Dave Peck. Determined to hunt him down, she and Ned split up and swept through the rooms of each of the three levels of the elegant club, searching every corner. Nancy was impressed by the vastness and extravagance.

The people were varied, from elegant to bizarre, exotic to all-American. Nancy looked at each one, her search for Dave dead-ending in an upstairs room that was lined with televisions all tuned to MTV. Ned was waiting for her there, and it was plain from his expression that he'd had no more luck than she had.

"No sign of him?" Nancy said.

Ned shook his head no.

"I saw a few people I knew, but not Dave. Vivian, Mr. Marshall's secretary, was down by the stage. And I saw Bess with Alan, not that she would talk to me." Nancy slumped down in an armchair and stared blankly at the checkerboard of television screens.

Ned sat down next to her. A heavy bass beat filled the room as a wild music video came to life on all the screens simultaneously.

The song faded, and a familiar Bent Fender tune came on. Nancy watched the screen a bit more attentively. The video cut from one scene to another, a collage of different shots. As Barton launched into the chorus of the song, a crowd scene came on, men and women emerging from a subway station. In the crowd were the members of Bent Fender themselves and several other people Nancy recognized. Linda Ferrare's cousin was there—the boy George had been dancing with the night before—and a woman who was the female lookalike of Mark Bailey, the guitarist. His sister, Nancy surmised.

Fender had chosen to use people they knew, rather than using actors to fill out the crowd. Nancy spotted Ann Nordquist, and her stomach did a nervous flip-flop. Her father and Ann were out again this evening.

But she forgot about them, her eyes suddenly glued to a television screen. Coming up the staircase on screen was a couple, kissing. The man was short. He had longish wavy brown hair and a familiar-looking, stocky, muscular physique. In amazement Nancy stepped up to the television screens.

"Ned, you won't believe this," she said slowly.

"What?"

"In a way . . . we did find Dave." Nancy pointed at the screen and at the same time tried to figure out who Dave was with. The girl's face was mostly hidden, but when the twosome reached the top of the staircase and pulled apart, Nancy let out a gasp. "I can't believe it! Ned, *look!* It's *Vivian!* What if she and Dave are a number off the screen as well as on!"

Instantly, Nancy was running. "Come on, Ned. Vivian was just downstairs. We have to find her."

Down the two flights of stairs Nancy flew, around the side of the dance floor and toward the stage where she had last seen Vivian. Ned was right behind her.

She scanned the mass of people, picking out the back of Vivian's jet-black coif. Marshall's secretary was in the wings to one side of the stage, talking to someone. The person leaned forward, into the light, and Nancy saw his scowling face. *Alan.* He moved his hands wildly, saying something Nancy couldn't hear.

Moving in closer, Nancy motioned to Ned to stay down below stage level where they wouldn't be seen. The dance music stopped. Linda Ferrare was tuning her bass. Mark Bailey was adjusting one of his guitar strings. A surge of excitement raced through the crowd as they waited for the band.

But Alan and Vivian continued to face off. "No!" Alan said furiously. Nancy and Ned were close enough now to make out what he was saying. "It's gotten totally out of control! I had no idea—"

"Save it, pest," Vivian interrupted. "You'll come around. I'm going to make absolutely sure of it."

"No way, Vivian. As soon as the concert is over, I'm going to tell Nancy everything.

"And what's more, I'm going to tell Bess too." Alan looked behind him. Nancy couldn't see through the dark curtain at the edge of the stage, but it was clear that Bess was back there, probably standing just out of earshot.

"But Alan," Vivian singsonged nastily, "if you tell Bess what you know, you'll have to admit that you lied about seeing Barton."

"I knew it!" Nancy exclaimed under her breath.

"Your precious angel won't like that one little bit," Vivian mocked.

"I can only hope she'll understand," Alan said. "I never should have believed your stories in the first place."

Nancy and Ned exchanged glances.

"The second I finish my last note, Vivian, you're through." Nancy could hear Alan's footsteps as he stormed away and took his place on stage.

"Don't count on it!" Vivian called out, her voice following him, and she let out a frightening laugh.

"What do you suppose she means by that?" Ned asked.

"I don't know, but I don't like the sound of it."

Nancy and Ned made their way to a table when they were out of Vivian's field of vision. By then the band had assembled on stage, their instruments fully tuned, their sound levels set.

Alan was watching Jim Parker, seated behind his keyboard console. Jim gave an almost imperceptible nod, and the band let their first chords wail.

They were halfway into their second number when Alan's amp began crackling with ear-piercing static. He stopped playing immediately and fiddled with some dials on the equipment. Suddenly, sparks spewed from one of the wires. Someone in the audience screamed. Then the equipment went dead—and the club was plunged into total darkness!

Chapter

Eleven

WHAT'S HAPPENING?" A girl shrieked. "Is it a hold-up or something?"

"No," someone else shouted. "It's a fire!"

"Fire?" a man yelled fearfully.

Mass confusion broke loose.

Separated from Ned, Nancy was jostled from two sides as she inched in what she hoped was the direction of the closest wall. She waved her arms in front of her until her hands found the smooth, solid plaster. Turning, she pressed her back to it, squeezing out of the way of the hordes of people making blind, panicked dashes in every direction.

"Simon? Simon, where are you?" a woman

near Nancy was screaming, her voice filled with terror. "Simon, are you all right?"

"Stay calm!" Nancy called out to her. "The lights will be back on in a few minutes."

"Simon!" the woman kept shrieking.

"Ladies and gentlemen, please do not panic." A new voice filled the air, loud and hollow. Someone was speaking through a megaphone. "The electrical short on stage caused a temporary power outage, but the electricity should be restored in a matter of minutes. Please stay where you are. I repeat, stay where you are."

Nancy eased herself into a sitting position on the floor to wait. She could hear others do the same. But as the panic subsided, her own fears began to blossom in the overwhelming blackness. Had the power outage been an accident? Or was it perhaps a little too convenient, coming as it did on the heels of Vivian's threat to Alan?

The minutes ticked away. Nancy prayed to herself that this would be no rerun of the night Barton disappeared. Then, suddenly, the power came flooding back on. Nancy blinked, needing to adjust her eyes even to the subdued lighting of the club. The band stood on stage, checking their instruments and amplifiers now that the electricity was working again. But one person was missing. Where was Alan?

Nancy felt panic rising in her throat. Then she noticed that the curtain shielding the backstage area from the audience had been pulled down, a casualty of the frenzied rush of people immediately following the blackout. She let out a noisy sigh of relief as she saw Alan standing off to one side, staring at a sheet of paper.

Ned was still more or less where he had been before the power had blown. As he looked around, Nancy waved to him. He caught sight of her, his face softening with relief, and made his way across the room. Nancy kissed him quickly.

"Listen, Ned," she said. "I'm going to go talk to Alan and see what he wanted to tell me. Maybe you should go look for George and make sure she's okay."

"What about Bess?" Ned wanted to know. "I don't see her back there." He looked behind the stage.

"I'll ask Alan about her."

"Meet you back here?" Ned asked.

"In ten minutes." Nancy hoisted herself onto the stage and headed straight for Alan. She wasn't bothered by any guards. They were trying to restore order in the club. The concert evening was over.

Alan stood rooted to the stage floor. He was staring blankly ahead of him, his cheeks pale, his eyes glazed. His right hand shook violently as he clutched his guitar.

"Hey," Nancy called out gently. "Alan."

He whipped his head around in her direction. "What?" he said, his voice as tight as a rubber band at the point of snapping.

"What's wrong?" Nancy moved to his side and touched his arm. The hollow look in his eyes made her almost afraid to hear his answer.

"Wrong? Why should anything be wrong?"

"I heard you arguing with Vivian."

Alan inhaled sharply but said nothing.

"I know you didn't really see Barton," Nancy prodded, "so why don't you tell me the rest?"

Alan shook his head back and forth, never lifting his eyes to meet Nancy's. "No. No, I can't. You wouldn't understand." Nancy sensed the terror behind the stubborn words.

"How am I supposed to understand if you don't tell me?" she asked. Only a short time before he had seemed so determined to let her in on whatever he knew. What horrible thing had happened while the lights were out to make him change his mind so completely?

"Alan," Nancy persisted, "that blackout happened for a reason, didn't it?"

"Please," Alan begged, "I said I'm not talking."

"Okay. I can't force you. But at least tell me where Bess is. I thought she was back here."

Alan bit down hard on his lower lip, and Nancy could see it tremble.

"Oh, *Alan!*" Nancy cried. "It isn't Bess, is it?" She held her breath. Alan didn't utter a sound. "Alan!"

"She's fine," he whispered hoarsely. "Bess is fine."

111

"Where is she?" Nancy felt like a five-gear car being forced to run in first.

"She's sick. She went back to the hotel."

"Alone?"

"She took a taxi."

"How'd she get out of here so fast? The lights just came back on. Besides, I saw her when I got here, and she looked fine." Nancy reached for Alan's shoulders and started shaking him. "What's wrong with her? Tell me!"

"Hey, give me a break," he protested weakly, stepping back. "She left by the back door—had a cold or the flu or something, and she specifically asked that no one disturb her later tonight." Nancy listened to Alan's story gain momentum. "She went back to the hotel to take some cold medicine and go to sleep, okay? Are you finished giving me the third degree?"

Nancy let her arms drop. "You mean Bess went home to take her Motocillan?"

"Motocillan. That's right."

"Are you sure?"

"Of course I'm sure."

Nancy shivered, despite the warm air inside the club. "Alan," she said coldly, "if Bess ever took Motocillan, she could die. She's allergic to it. Now tell me the truth."

The guitar slid out of Alan's hand. His knees gave out, and he slumped to the floor.

"I can't. I can't. If I tell they'll . . ."

"Who's they?" Nancy fought to stay calm. "Is

there anyone here you're afraid of?" She motioned to the members of Bent Fender, who had gathered around nervously when they'd seen Alan collapse.

Alan shook his head.

"Then how is anyone going to know you told us?" Nancy asked softly.

"Because you'll try to find her . . ."

"Bess? Then she's not back at the hotel." Nancy's voice hardened. "Alan, what's going on?"

Alan's words came out in a jumbled rush. "You can't go after her—the shipment—they'll hurt her if the shipment doesn't go out tonight. Please, just let them get it out . . ."

"What shipment? Alan, I swear, I'd never do anything to harm Bess. You've got to believe me."

Alan sighed deeply. "They grabbed her," he rasped, "during the blackout so I wouldn't tell you what I heard. I don't know where they took her."

"Who's they? Vivian? Mr. Marshall?"

"Marshall?" Puzzled, Alan looked up. "No, not him."

"You mean Vivian's in on this, but Harold Marshall isn't?"

"That witch," Alan said through clenched teeth. "Everyone thinks Marshall is the boss, but Vivian's got him running around in circles, and he's too stupid and egotistical to realize it. He's like a marionette, and she's pulling all the strings."

"Of course!" Nancy nodded grimly. "How could we have been so blind? Roger, remember you said Vivian would do anything for Marshall? She buttered him up until she had complete control over him. Marshall's huge ego made him take credit for all the ideas she fed him, which was exactly what Vivian wanted. That way, if anyone caught on to what she was doing, her boss would shoulder the blame. I almost fell for it too."

"It's an easy mistake to make," Roger said. "Marshall's personality doesn't exactly make you want to give him the benefit of the doubt." His mouth settled into a tight line. "Although he did offer you that record contract, didn't he?" Roger turned to Alan.

Alan hesitated.

"You promise that nothing will happen to Bess if I tell you?" Alan asked again.

"Alan, we're all Bess's friends," Nancy assured him. "I know she and I had that fight, but I love Bess. If anything happens to her—"

"Okay. You were right to think that Marshall offered me the contract just to get me to tell you I'd seen Barton. But I didn't think about that, just like I didn't realize that Marshall's offer was *Vivian's* idea. I didn't see anything I didn't want to see. I was so wrapped up in the idea of being famous . . ." Alan pounded his fist against the floor. "This whole thing is my fault. If I hadn't been so convinced I was star material, Bess would be safe right now."

"Alan, this is no time to start blaming yourself," Nancy said firmly. "You have to tell us what you know so we can figure out what to do about it."

"I really believed them. I thought they wanted me to record because they thought I was good. And when Marshall told me that Barton's disappearance was a publicity stunt, I believed that, too. I mean, I *wanted* to believe it. As long as he was all right, but out of the picture, he was my ticket to success. So when Harold Marshall asked me to tell you I saw Barton, I agreed. Don't get me wrong. I really believed Barton was fine."

"But Alan, I thought you said Marshall didn't have anything to do with whatever is going on," said Nancy, confused.

"That's right. He didn't. Vivian planted the publicity idea in his head and then told him she'd take care of the details. So when you started asking questions, Nancy, he thought you were nosing in where you didn't belong. Vivian convinced him to offer me a contract in exchange for getting you off his back. Of course, neither of them ever expected to let me go through with the recording." Alan toyed with a strand of dark curly hair. "I guess I was a fool."

"Alan," Nancy asked impatiently, "how do you know all this?"

"I'm getting to that. See, I had convinced myself that my lie about Barton wouldn't hurt anyone, but when you and Bess had that fight, I saw that something was wrong. To make things worse, Bess was defending me when I didn't even deserve it."

"Why didn't you level with her right then and there? And with me?" Nancy bent down to look Alan in the eye.

"I wanted to. But I was so afraid Bess would hate me for it. I just didn't have the guts to confess." Regret was etched on his face, and Nancy felt her anger toward him soften a bit.

"So I stuck to my lie," Alan went on, "but I just didn't feel right about it after that. You started me worrying about whether Barton really was all right, and I realized that if anything happened to him, it would be partially my fault. I still couldn't bring myself to tell Bess then, but I decided that, at the very least, I ought to go to Mr. Marshall and insist that I see Barton in person. Just to know for sure." Alan took a breath.

"Anyhow, I went over to his office late this afternoon, while Bess was out jogging. He wasn't there, but Vivian was. She was sitting in his office using the telephone, and the door was open a crack. I could hear everything she said, and it was what I just told you about the publicity story and my record contract."

"And something about a shipment of some sort?" Nancy asked, recalling his earlier words.

"Yeah. I don't know what kind of shipment, but she told whoever she was talking to that it was going out tonight."

"The bootleg albums," Nancy said. "Did she say where they were being shipped to?"

"Heading east, that's all."

"Weird," Roger said. "I thought New York was as far east as you could get. Maybe she meant the east side of town."

"Or maybe she wasn't talking about this country at all," Nancy said. "Maybe by east she meant the eastern hemisphere."

"Like China?" Roger asked.

"Exactly," Nancy sighed. Her hunch about the lack of copyright laws in that country could very well play out. But that didn't make her feel any better. It meant that Ann Nordquist might not be off the hook after all.

However, any further thoughts about China and Ann Nordquist ceased when Alan began talking again. "I don't know if the destination is going to matter much when you hear the rest of Vivian's conversation," he said.

"Oh no." Nancy steeled herself for what was next.

"Vivian said that there was a body going out with the shipment."

"Barton!" Roger Gold exclaimed in horror.

"Tell me Vivian's exact words," Nancy instructed Alan, her heart filling with dread.

Alan tensed. "Like I said, 'one body going out with the shipment,' was the way she put it. Then the person on the other end of the phone must have said something. Vivian answered, 'No, we're going to do it right before we ship him out—silence him for good.'" Alan's voice was shaking again. "The last thing I heard was, 'Yeah, pick up at the duck house, as usual. Ten-thirty. Right.' Then Vivian hung up."

Nancy glanced at her watch. Nine o'clock. "What happened next?" she said, her own voice trembling. If she couldn't find Barton in an hour and a half, she might never find him—*alive*—or find Bess either!

"I tried to sneak out," Alan said, "but I was so freaked out about what I'd overheard that I knocked something over as I was leaving the outer office—a chair, I think. After that, I just ran as fast as I could, down the stairs and out the building. I went to the hotel and got Bess and brought her here to the club. I thought I got away clean."

"But you didn't tell Bess what you'd heard?" Nancy asked.

Alan shook his head. "I knew I had to tell you everything—tonight, I thought, here at the club —so I figured I'd level with Bess at the same time. Besides, I guess I wanted to put that part off as long as possible, having Bess find out she'd fallen for a worthless bum."

"But how did Vivian find out you knew?" Nancy asked.

Alan reddened. "Vivian looked out the window and saw me leaving. She knew she'd find me here at the concert."

"So she arranged the power outage and had Bess kidnapped to keep you from talking?" Nancy asked, beginning to put all the pieces together.

Alan stood up, reached into the back pocket of his leather pants, and pulled out a crinkled piece of yellow lined paper. Silently, he handed it to Nancy.

She smoothed it out and read the words printed in bold, box letters. *DO NOT SAY A WORD TO ANYONE IF YOU WANT TO SEE YOUR GIRLFRIEND AGAIN,* the note read.

Chapter

Twelve

WHO GAVE THIS to you?" Nancy demanded, waving the note.

"Someone pulled me off stage and pressed it into my hand while the lights were out," Alan explained.

"What I don't get is why they didn't just take Alan." Roger said.

"I think they realized that if Alan vanished before this show, like Barton did before the last one, it was going to look pretty suspicious. And they wouldn't have such an easy time explaining it the second time around."

"I wish they *had* taken me," Alan said. "I

didn't mean for anyone to get hurt. I was so busy dreaming about how famous I'd be. If anything happens to Bess—or Barton—"

"We've got to find out where they're shipping from," Nancy put in, "and get there fast!"

"But you can't look for her!" Alan's voice rang out. "You promised. If they realize you're coming after them, who knows what they'll do to Bess!"

"Alan, think about it," Nancy said, barely able to face the facts herself. "We don't have any choice. You heard Vivian's plans for Barton. If we don't go after them, there may be two bodies going out with the albums."

"What are we going to do?" Anguish was written all over Alan's face.

"We're going to get ourselves out of this madness out here," Nancy said, determined. "And then we're going to find that duck house Vivian mentioned."

A few moments later, Nancy was running her index finger down the listings in a telephone book. "Duck House. Let's see. D-U-B, D-U-C . . . Duck. The Duck's Back, Duck Floor Coverings, Duck Sport and Leisure Shop. No Duck House." She slammed the heavy book shut. "Any luck, George?"

George shook her head. She was bent over the yellow pages. "No pet stores with that name. Maybe duck house isn't the *name* of the place, just a place that has duck."

"How about stores that specialize in aquariums and water habitats?" Alan suggested.

"You'd be more likely to find goldfish there," Nancy said.

"There are tons of pet stores listed that specialize in birds," George said. "Not that we'd have any idea which ones to go to first."

"Maybe we should divide up," Roger Gold suggested. "There are enough of us to cover a pretty big area."

With the concert postponed, the members of Bent Fender had gathered with Nancy, Alan, Ned, and George in the private office of the club manager, to try to come up with a rescue plan.

"Well, it's true, there are plenty of us," Nancy said, "but if we split up, I don't see how one or two of us is going to be much of a match for a gang of killers. Besides, like George said, who knows if 'the duck house' has anything to do with pet shops at all? It's just a shot in the dark."

"But it's the only shot we've come up with so far," Alan reminded her anxiously. "Listen, there's 'Jungle Paradise,' 'Birds of a Feather,' 'Hot House Exotic Birds' . . ."

"Somehow, I don't exactly think a duck is considered an exotic bird." Nancy's mouth settled into a grim line.

"Or even a pet, really." Linda Ferrare spoke up.

"The truth is, I kind of think of it as something to eat. You know, like Peking duck," Roger Gold put in. "What a time to be thinking about food," he said with a rueful smile.

"Roger!" Nancy jumped out of the lounge chair she had been sitting in. "Say that again."

"What? What a time to be thinking about food?"

"No, before that."

"Peking duck?"

"That's it! Why didn't I think of it right away?"

Ned put a hand on Nancy's shoulder. "You want to let the rest of us in on it, Nan?"

"The Duck House, the lack of copyright laws in Mainland China, James Lee." Nancy reeled off a list of clues.

"James Lee. You mean Dave Peck's boss?" Ned asked. "I still don't get it."

"Don't you see? Mrs. Peck said James Lee's brother had taken her and Dave to a restaurant his brother owned, right? What if 'Lee' is the Chinese last name. It could even be 'Li.' Remember, we've never seen it spelled."

"You mean Dave's boss might be the connection to China. And Ann Nordquist isn't mixed up in all of this?" Ned asked.

"Exactly," Nancy affirmed. "China just might be his native country, and the place where he still has black-market contacts." She grabbed the yellow pages and thumbed through them. "All right! Roger, you did it! You hit the nail on the head! Here it is! Li's Duck House in Chinatown!" She clapped triumphantly. "Bess and Barton, here we come!"

Nancy got out of the cab that had sped her to the restaurant. Ned, George, and Alan got out too. Another taxi behind them dropped off Roger, Linda, Jim, and Mark.

Across the street was a four-story building. The windows of the top two floors were boarded up. The two lower floors were bright with lighted windows, through which Nancy could see diners seated at tables laden with tureens and platters of food. A deep red facade decorated the lower level, with a sign above the entrance spelling out "Li's Duck House." Sure enough, the L of Li's was formed from the tail of an ornate dragon.

"That cinches it!" Nancy announced, pointing to the sign. "That L on the dragon, it must be a sort of calling card for Li and everybody who works for him. I'm sure the limo Dave was in belongs to him, too."

She strode toward the curb. But Ned followed and caught hold of her arm. "Nan, the people who have Bess and Barton aren't playing games. Don't you think we should wait for the police to get here? Sergeant Wald said—"

Nancy had telephoned the police just before leaving the club and arranged for them to meet her at Li's Duck House. She could still hear Sergeant Wald's words ringing in her ears. "The Li gang is involved in everything from gambling to smuggling. Watch out, kid. They're dangerous."

"No," Nancy answered firmly. "We have to get Bess and Barton out of there! The sergeant and his officers will be our backup."

"But we can't very well waltz into that restaurant and ask them to turn Bess and Barton over," George said sensibly.

"That's why the rest of you are going to wait here while I go scout out the building."

"Nancy," Ned said sternly, "remember what you said earlier. If it comes down to one of us against a whole gang of them, it won't be much of a match."

"It won't come down to that."

"At least let me come with you," Alan spoke up. "I was the one who got us into this mess, at least in part, so let me help you get us out."

"Well, okay. Maybe it would be safer for two of us to go in."

Once inside the restaurant, Nancy breathed in the warm, spicy-smelling odor, then gave a quick but thorough look around. Most of the dozen tables were occupied by diners. In the rear, the kitchen was partially visible through the windows of swinging metal doors. To one side was a flight of stairs going up and another flight going down. A sign for the restrooms and telephones hung over an arrow pointing downstairs.

"Two for dinner?" A woman approached Nancy and Alan, holding out menus.

"Oh, ah, would you mind if I used your restroom?" Nancy asked politely.

The woman frowned. "Customers only," she said coldly.

"My uncle eats here every week," Nancy lied. Her blood was running cold, but she flashed her warmest smile. "A tall man, gray hair and a mustache. I was here with him just last Sunday."

The woman stood aside. "All right," she said grudgingly, "go ahead."

Nancy glanced at the clock located over the metal swinging doors. It was already a quarter to ten, and she had only until ten-thirty to find Bess. That left only forty-five minutes—and time was running out fast!

Chapter

Thirteen

THE HOSTESS TURNED away, and Nancy tugged at Alan's sleeve. "We've got to hurry! When no one's looking, go up to the next floor and see what you can find. Look for another staircase. I'm going to check out the downstairs, but so many people have access to it, I think the top floors are our best bet."

Alan grabbed Nancy's hand and squeezed it warmly. When the coast was clear, he headed for the stairs.

In the basement, Nancy found an open space with two wall telephones and a shabby sofa. Off this area were two tiny restrooms and a closed door. The door opened easily. Behind it was a large boiler, water pipes, a central heating unit, old kitchenware, and a walk-in refrigerator. Wall shelves were lined with cans of Chinese ingredients. But there was no sign of either the two prisoners or a shipment of records.

Nancy raced back up the steps. Then, unnoticed, she went up the next flight. She found Alan standing at the edge of the second-floor dining room. "No luck" was the meaning of the look they gave each other.

Waiters were carrying food to the customers from a dumbwaiter that was positioned on one wall. The staircase Nancy had come up ended there, and she saw no exits that could have led to the third floor. She surveyed the ceiling, looking for a trap door.

Nothing.

Alan gave her a helpless shrug. "Maybe people going upstairs use *that.*" He pointed to a dumbwaiter, half-concealed by a partition.

Nancy gave him a look. "I suppose, if you're prepared to tie yourself up like a pretzel."

"Sorry. It was a dumb suggestion." Alan sighed. "But how else do you get to those top floors?"

"There's got to be a way. They can't possibly move heavy loads of record albums down on a dumbwaiter." *Not to mention moving down a body—or two bodies.*

Don't think of Barton and Bess as "bodies,"

Nancy scolded herself, but she sensed Alan was thinking the same thing. She glanced at her watch. It was coming on to ten o'clock, scarcely more than half an hour before pickup. If nothing had gone wrong, Bess and Barton were alive and somewhere in the building. But where?

Nancy looked around once more at the people enjoying their dinners under a tapestry depicting a serene waterfall. It hurt her to watch life going on as usual while Bess's and Barton's lives were still at stake.

The tapestry! Suddenly Nancy realized what she'd missed on her first look around the room. "Follow me," she whispered urgently to Alan. She moved toward the tapestry, which decorated the wall opposite the windows she'd seen when she'd gotten out of the taxi. As she and Alan crossed the room she discreetly put a hand to her left ear and removed one of her blue teardrop earrings, which she then dropped into her shirt pocket.

"Excuse me," she said to a couple at one of the tables beneath the woven wall hanging, then gestured toward Alan. "My friend and I had dinner at this table earlier in the evening, and I think I might have dropped an earring. Do you mind if I take a look?"

"Go right ahead," said a silver-haired man, getting up from his chair to allow Nancy to look behind the table.

Quickly, she bent down and grasped one of the bottom corners of the tapestry. When she lifted it up, she saw a window. That was it! The rear of the building faced the next street. There was probably a second entrance at the back. All she had to do was go around to the next block to find the door to the top two floors.

"What are you doing?" the man asked. "How could your earring possibly get behind the tapestry?"

"I'm sorry. No time to explain." Nancy took Alan's arm and tore down the stairs and out of the building, leaving the man to stare after them.

The plain brown truck sat outside the other side of the building, the cab doors open. "All ready to load in the albums," George hissed to Nancy as she and the others peered around the corner of the block.

"Not just the albums," Nancy said with grave apprehension. "We can't wait for the police any longer. We've got to move in right now."

"But what about that heavyset man at the door?" Roger said. "He might be armed."

At that moment, the guard stubbed out the end of the cigarette he'd been smoking and pulled open the door he had been standing in front of. A short man in dark clothes came out carrying a large crate.

"Dave!" Nancy whispered. "With a load of albums!"

"But they're early. They weren't supposed to start until ten-thirty," Alan said.

"I know," Nancy replied grimly. "We've got even less time than we thought. Where on earth is Sergeant Wald? When Dave brings down the last box, Bess and Barton are through." Dave put the crate into the truck. Behind him, a taller heavyset man came out with another crate, and then a third man emerged. The tall man fit the description the Radio City Music Hall guards had given of the man who had been Dave's partner.

"Okay, guys, listen up," Nancy said, gathering everyone around. "We have to put Dave and his pals out of commission for a while. There are more of us than them, so if we take them by surprise, it shouldn't be too tough. Once we're inside, we'll break into groups to look for Bess and Barton."

"What if more of those creeps are inside?" Mark Bailey asked.

"Then we'd better pray their hands are full of crates and that we're faster than they are," Nancy replied uneasily. "Now, I'm going to go ask Mr. Muscles over there for a cigarette." She pointed toward the guard. "While he's holding the match for me, I'm going to practice a new move we learned in karate."

Nancy rounded the corner, walking slowly toward the guarded door.

The guard watched Nancy's progress down the

narrow, empty side street. He shifted uneasily when she made eye contact and gave him a tentative smile.

"Can you spare a smoke?" she asked, hoping her voice sounded normal.

Arching a bushy eyebrow, the guard looked down the block, which was home to a handful of grocery stores that were closed for the night. Then he put a hand into his jacket pocket and pulled out a red and white box. After giving Nancy a cigarette, he fished around in another pocket for a book of matches.

Nancy was close enough to make out the L-tailed dragon on the matchbook. James Li again. She put the cigarette in her mouth. The guard held a lit match with one hand, cupping the other around the flame as Nancy bent forward and edged the tip of the cigarette toward the light. Then, in one brisk, split-second movement, she smashed the heel of her hand into the guard's chin. He didn't even have a chance to shout before he fell to the pavement.

"Ned, Roger," she called out. "Quick. Give me a hand." They hoisted the unconscious guard into the back of the truck. Then they waited behind the door to the building. When Dave and his cohorts reappeared, they jumped them.

Dave fought free from the surprise attack. Nancy brought her right arm up for a blow, but he caught hold and pinned it behind her back, twisting painfully. By then, though, the others had appeared. George and Alan helped Nancy overpower Dave, while Linda, Mark, and Jim gave Roger and Ned a hand in carrying the other two, still kicking and fighting, into the back of the truck.

They finally shoved Dave in too and slammed the back door shut. With her left arm, Nancy snapped closed several padlocks that were attached to it, imprisoning the four men in their own vehicle. "There. That ought to hold them for a while." Nancy allowed herself a second to inspect her twisted right shoulder. She could hardly lift her arm, and she massaged the soreness with her other hand.

"Nancy, you're hurt!" George observed anxiously.

"It's not that bad." Nancy said, steeling herself against the pain.

"Are you sure?"

Nancy managed a stiff smile in spite of the throbbing in her shoulder. "Okay," she said, "someone better wait down here for the police while we go in. Alan, will you volunteer?"

"I'll do whatever you say."

"Good. If you have any trouble, yell. The rest of you, follow me."

Inside, they groped their way up two dark, narrow flights of stairs and then split up, Ned and George exploring the third floor with Nancy, the musicians taking the top level.

"What a place to get stuck in without a flashlight," George muttered as their group inched forward blindly.

With Ned and George behind her, Nancy guided herself along the wall of what apparently was a narrow hallway. Suddenly her hand slid around a corner. The hallway had ended. "I think we're in a big room," Nancy whispered. "There's got to be a light switch somewhere near here."

"Pay dirt!" came Ned's voice, as fluorescent overhead lamps illuminated a huge loft space.

"Wow!" Nancy looked around her in amazement. The loft was filled with the best, most modern recording equipment available.

"Nancy! Ned! George!" It was Roger calling from above them down the staircase. "We found them! Hurry!"

The recording equipment forgotten, the three friends followed Roger's voice, racing upstairs and through another loft littered with cartons like the ones Dave and his cohorts had been carrying.

"In here!" Roger peered out from a smaller room partitioned off at the very back of the loft.

"Nancy!" cried Bess as Linda, Mark, and Jim finished untying the ropes that had bound her and Barton. "George! Ned!" Bess was on her feet, hugging them all at once. "I can't believe you found us! I thought I was never going to see any of you again!"

Nancy pulled Bess close with her left arm,

warm tears of relief trickling down both friends' cheeks. Nancy squeezed her as hard as she could. "Oh, Bess, thank heavens we got here in time!"

"I'll say," Barton Novak agreed tremulously. The members of Bent Fender were having their own reunion.

"Barton, are you okay? Did they hurt you?" Linda asked.

"Well, spending two days tied to a chair isn't my idea of a vacation." Barton grinned.

Bess was less ready to laugh off their near brush with death. "Oh, Nan, to think I didn't believe a single word you told me," she cried. "Barton was in this awful place, just like you said, and they were going to kill us . . ." Her sentence dissolved into sobs.

"It's okay, Bess," Nancy consoled her. "Everything's going to be fine."

"No it's not. I was so rotten to you. How can you ever forgive me. I apologize a million, trillion times."

"Hey, no need."

"Boy, just wait until I get my hands on that double-crossing liar Alan Wales."

"Wait a minute, Bess," Nancy said, surprising herself. "Don't be so hard on the guy. His biggest crime was just being swept away by his dreams."

"I don't know, Nancy. Those dreams almost got Barton and me murdered!" Bess paused. "So where is the rat, anyway?"

"Downstairs waiting for the police."

"You're very much mistaken," an unfamiliar male voice boomed out behind Nancy. "The police are downstairs in the basement, locked to the pipes with their own handcuffs."

Nancy whirled around to see a small man dressed in a neat gray suit, with a dark hat pulled low over his face. He held a gun. And the gun was pointed directly at Nancy!

The man smiled a bone-chilling, evil smile. "James Li at your service," he announced. "The next person who moves is dead."

Chapter

Fourteen

MAY I EXTEND my congratulations, Miss Drew? You almost put a damper on my little party. Almost, but not quite." James Li gave a demonic laugh. "It is Miss Drew, isn't it?" He touched the tip of her nose with the cold, hard barrel of his gun.

The tap of high-heeled shoes sounded on the bare floor behind James Li. "That's Nancy Drew all right." Vivian stepped out of the shadows, Dave by her side. "This'll teach you to go poking around in business that doesn't concern you," she said.

Nancy remained silent, not giving Vivian the satisfaction of an answer.

"It's a pity my little warning the other night failed to scare you off," Li offered.

"That knife-throwing act was yours?" Nancy asked, an edge of bitterness to her voice.

"Through one of my boys."

"Lucky for me he missed."

"Lucky, Miss Drew? I told you it was just a warning. Otherwise . . ." The look in James Li's cold dark eyes more than finished the sentence. Nancy knew this man played for keeps. "Alas, it seems only the inevitable was delayed." Li smiled. "Did you really think you could stop us? I knew something was wrong tonight as soon as I saw your budding rock-and-roll star standing at the entrance instead of my guard, Petey. When Vivian told me who the young man was, we realized you must have traced us here. But no matter. I let my boys out of the truck, they told us the police were on their way, and we simply waited inside the entrance for your friend Sergeant Wald and his brave men in blue."

"But what did you do to Alan?" Bess demanded. "Not that I really care," she added unconvincingly.

James Li frowned. "A minor setback. He managed to get away while we were attending to the officers. But some of my boys went after him. He won't get far. As for the rest of you, I'll give you a chance to say your goodbyes to each other."

"How nice of you," muttered George.

"Once the truck is loaded," Li continued, "we're going to send you on a one-way trip."

Bess let out a choked cry.

"Don't worry, he won't get away with this," Nancy said.

"I wouldn't place any bets on that, Miss Drew. Dave, tie them up."

One by one, Dave pushed the prisoners down into hard, straight-back chairs, bound their wrists and ankles, and secured them to the chairs with more rope. He saved Nancy for last, pulling the rope extra tight. A shooting pain seared through her injured arm.

"That's for practicing your karate moves on me," he said, sneering.

"It evens the score," Nancy said through gritted teeth, "for that rap on the head at the concert. You were the one who hit me, weren't you, Dave?" She tried to keep a hard look on her face in spite of the burning pain in her shoulder. Ned also eyed Dave angrily. If he got the chance, he'd pay Dave back for hurting Nancy.

Nancy could hear the sounds of boxes being carried down the stairs. It was as if the boxes were sand in an hourglass. When the boxes were gone, it would be all over.

Li fired off more orders. "Okay, Dave, you help the boys finish loading up. Vivian, you take this gun and keep it pointed at our guests. If they so much as breathe too loudly, let them have it.

I'm going down to the ship to tell them to start the motors."

"The ship that's going to carry the records?" Nancy asked.

"And Vivian and my boys and me." James Li smiled. "There isn't a thing you can do to stop us. I'm not thrilled about leaving the States, but once Mr. Novak here caught on to what we were doing, things got a little too hot to handle. I decided to make one more big shipment and then leave the country until things cooled off. It was unfortunate that I had to wait until tonight before doing away with him, but I couldn't risk having his body found before I was safely aboard ship."

"Then Alan found out about your plans right before the final shipment," Nancy said. "But you were afraid the disappearance of a second Fender guitarist would attract too much attention right before the critical night."

"Very perceptive of you, Miss Drew. We didn't want the police alerted."

"But we were able to coax the story out of Alan . . . and contact the police. You didn't count on that."

"No," Li agreed. "But it didn't pose much of a problem in the end, did it?" His mouth spread in a frightening smile. "And now, ladies and gentlemen, it's time for me to say good night." He tipped his hat. "Dave, you know what to do once the truck is loaded." He looked back at Nancy. "You see, there's going to be a tragic fire in this warehouse. But then, I'm sure my brother won't mind collecting insurance on the building while we're out of the country, lying low. And the diners downstairs will certainly leave at the first sign of smoke. It's just a shame you people on the upper floor will be trapped." Li laughed cruelly. "All right, go ahead, Dave. I'll meet you at the ship when you're through."

"You're leaving *now?*" Confusion registered on Dave's face. "But we had a deal. I'd take care of the records. You'd take care of the people."

"Correct. That was our arrangement. But I'm changing the deal. I don't like dirty work, and I want to be far away while it's being done. Do you understand?"

"But boss, I can't. I've never . . . I mean, I know this guy." Dave pointed to Ned, horrified as he realized what Li expected him to do. "He was my friend, kind of."

"Dave, I am going down to the dock. We'll be pulling anchor in twenty minutes, record albums or no record albums. The police will be looking for their men as soon as they discover they're missing. If you want to stay around and visit the prison wards, fine. If you want passage on my ship for yourself and your girlfriend," he looked at Vivian, "you'd better do as I say." James Li turned on his heel. But heading out the door, he was intercepted by Petey, the guard Nancy had asked for the light.

"Hey, boss?" Petey said. "We got a problem. It's that kid. We looked everywhere for him. I don't know how he got away so quick. It's like he just vanished or something."

Li tapped his pistol nervously against his palm. "Well then, you'd better hurry with those albums. He might get to the cops."

Petey nodded.

"You too, Dave," Li commanded. "Get to work."

"But—"

"That's the end of the discussion." Li headed out.

Dave looked around at Nancy and the others. "Viv, what do you think?"

"You mean about them? I think we better do what Li says," Vivian told him. "I don't have any intention of winding up in jail."

"I guess." Dave handed her his gun (with some reluctance, Nancy thought), and went into the next room to move the crates of albums.

"Vivian, you're not really going to listen to James Li, are you?" With her hands tied behind her back, Nancy had no option other than to try to talk Vivian out of the drastic plan. She suspected that Vivian was the person to convince. Dave was clearly shaken up at the thought of being responsible for so much bloodshed. If

Vivian changed her mind, Nancy was certain that Dave would go along with her. "You wouldn't really set that fire," Nancy said.

"A lot you know," Vivian replied roughly. "Before Dave introduced me to Jimmy Li, every nickel I earned from my lousy job went toward the rent on a one-room dump. I never had fancy clothes or went to nice restaurants or owned real jewelry."

"And now you have it all?"

"These aren't rhinestones on my finger, sweetheart." Vivian flashed a sparkling ring of gold and diamonds.

"But are all those luxuries worth having murder on your conscience for the rest of your life? Think about it. We're talking about human lives."

"I know what we're talking about." Vivian's voice was deadly cold.

"Look, it's no longer just a question of stealing masters or illegally copying albums or even knocking me out backstage at the Music Hall," Nancy said desperately. "You must be pretty loyal to James Li to kill for him."

"He takes good care of Dave and me."

"Vivian, how long have you known him?"

"Dave introduced me to him a few months ago, when he needed to get on the inside at World Communications. But I don't see what difference that makes."

"And Dave hasn't worked for him very long, either."

"They started doing business when Dave worked at Emerson Record World."

"That was less than a year ago," Ned put in.

"And you're ready to put yourself entirely in the hands of someone you've known for such a short time?" Nancy asked. "A man who makes deals and then 'changes' them as it suits him? Vivian, you and Dave are planning on escaping to a country where you don't know a soul except Mr. Li. You don't speak the language, you don't know any of the customs. Without that man, you're lost. And he's ready to let you carry out murder, so that he isn't responsible for it."

Vivian seemed to be considering Nancy's words. But then her face hardened. "You don't really care what happens to Dave and me. You're just pleading for your own lives. Well, you all deserve exactly what you get. We had a great thing going, and you came along and messed it up."

Dave poked his head into the room. "We're about to bring the last load down."

Nancy drew in a sharp, frightened breath. This was it.

"Good," Vivian said. "The sooner we get this over with, the better."

"Vivian, please," Nancy begged as Dave headed down the stairs with the crate. *"Please . . ."*

"Save it for the guy at the pearly gates." Vivian waved her gun menacingly.

"I guess this is goodbye," George managed to choke out. Nancy had never seen steely-nerved George shed a tear. She dropped her head, expecting the gunshot. But instead, she heard an ear-shattering scream!

Chapter

Fifteen

NANCY JERKED HER head up to see Vivian drenched in a steaming liquid. And wrestling the gun from her hand was . . .

"Alan!" Nancy cried out. "How on earth?"

Alan stood behind Vivian, holding her gun in one hand and a huge bowl in the other. "Hot egg drop soup," he grinned. Working swiftly, he untied his friends. "I figured the last place those muscle-brains would look for me was in their own building. I sneaked back in through the restaurant side and came up the dumbwaiter. You were right, Nancy. It was *not* the most comfortable ride." Alan unknotted the last bonds.

"Alan," Nancy said gratefully, "without you, we'd—"

"—never have gotten into this mess in the first place. The least I could do was save your skin."

Before Nancy could reply, footsteps on the stairs signaled Dave's return. "Okay, guys," she whispered. "You're going to have to take Li's henchmen on your own. I'm afraid my shoulder's given out on me."

"I thought you said it was fine," George scolded her.

"So I lied. I don't think I'm up for any fancy karate moves."

"It's all right, Nancy," said Roger Gold. "Even without you, it's nine of us against four of them."

Suddenly, Dave appeared in the room along with Li's other bullies. "Hey, what's going on? Viv, what are you doing on the fl—"

Dave caught a right to his jaw before the word was out of his mouth. The small room reverberated with sounds of punches, kicks, and heated exclamations.

It didn't take long for Nancy's friends to overpower Li's cohorts. "Good job," Nancy said breathlessly. "Alan, go down and see about those policemen. Take Vivian's gun, just in case."

Alan left the room and a few seconds later reappeared with four men in blue uniforms.

"Sergeant Wald," Nancy said, pointing to Dave, Vivian, and the other three men, "we have a little present for you. But there's one more. The boss, James Li. He's trying to escape on a ship that's about to pull anchor. Li told his boys he'd leave without the merchandise if he had to. Do you think we can stop him?"

"That should be easy." Sergeant Wald stepped forward. "Just tell us what dock he's leaving from, and we can radio headquarters. They'll have cars and a special navy unit over there in no time."

Nancy turned toward Li's little gang, now securely tied with the ropes that had held her and her friends just moments earlier. "Okay, which one of you wants to tell me where your boss is leaving from?"

Dave and the others remained silent.

"Do you think he'd do the same for you?" Nancy asked. "No way. He wouldn't stick his neck out one fraction of an inch. In fact, he's getting ready to leave without you right this second."

No answer.

"Dave, think about what James Li left you to do. He didn't want to do it himself, so who did he stick with it?"

Dave scowled. "Yeah, that bum."

"Come on, tell us," Nancy urged. She'd learned in karate class that a chain was most easily broken at its weakest link. "Maybe if you cooperate, they'll let you off with a lighter sentence."

"Don't listen to her," Vivian commanded.

Dave looked from his girlfriend to Nancy, and back to his girlfriend.

"You know, your mother would be heartbroken to see her son locked away forever," Nancy said, trying a different tack.

"How do you know what my mother would think?" Dave shouted.

"Ned had a little chat with her," Nancy replied calmly. "We were trying to track you down."

Dave's face went from furious to panicked. The chain snapped. "All right, you win. I'll tell you where he is."

Nancy allowed herself a long overdue sigh of relief.

She was safe. Bess and Barton were fine. And Li's gang was about to be put away. It was true that her shoulder ached, that her wrists and ankles were sore where Dave had tied them, and that her head was still bruised from where he had hit her the first night. But she had never in her life felt happier or more alive!

That happy feeling was still with Nancy the next morning as she flounced down on the edge of Bess's bed. She steadied herself with her left arm, since her right one was still sore from the previous night. "Come on, lazybones! Do you want to sleep through your last day in New York?"

Bess groaned and pulled the covers over her head.

"Bess!" Nancy jostled her friend's leg through the blanket. "It's almost eleven o'clock."

Bess peeked one half-open eye out from her cocoon. "Nan, don't you know that people who've been through traumas need lots of rest?" She rolled over on her stomach.

"You seemed just fine at our midnight celebration supper. Remember putting away all those spare ribs?"

George came out of the bathroom, a towel wrapped like a turban around her wet hair. "Don't even mention spare ribs. I ate enough last night for the rest of the week."

"And you're going to eat even more this afternoon at that luncheon the Chinatown Neighborhood Association is giving for us," Nancy reminded her. "Mrs. Chen, she's president of the association, told me that the community is incredibly grateful to all of us for helping to put James Li behind bars. What a bully! It wasn't enough for him to pirate records and run all those other big-time illegal operations the police told us he had going. No, he had to muscle in on the small businesses in Chinatown, too."

"Yeah, I can certainly understand why the community is so glad to see him go," George said. "And it's really nice of them to give us an honorary luncheon. But I don't know if I'm going to be able to touch it." She patted her lean, flat stomach.

"Don't worry. I'll help you out." Bess finally

sat up in bed and stretched her arms over her head.

George rolled her eyes. "Well, look who finally rises at the mention of her favorite sport— eating."

"Oh, come on, give me a break. How often do you get some of the best Chinese chefs this side of the Pacific to make a special meal just for you?"

"Not too often," George answered. "And speaking of not too often, there's something I've been wanting to ask you, Bess."

"Yeah?"

"Alan said he went down to World Communications yesterday while you were out jogging. Since when have you turned into a jock?"

Bess made a face. "We-e-ell . . . I sort of ended up doing more shopping than jogging . . ."

"Figures," George said. "So how much did that little jog cost you?"

Bess cringed. "I don't think I should say."

"Come on, spill it. What'd you blow?"

Bess pouted. "George, don't tell me you've never gone out on a spur-of-the-moment shopping spree. How about that time you bought all those weights from the sports shop to use at home, and then you joined the gym, so you don't even *need* your own weights?"

George frowned. "Well, at least I don't go out running with a shopping bag and my wallet."

Nancy sighed. "Okay, you two. No more arguing. From now on, this vacation's going to be fun, fun, fun."

"Famous last words," George said.

Nancy shot George a mock glare. "Don't even think it," she said. "It *is* going to be a vacation. Even if it's for just one more day."

"Yeah, I wouldn't mind some fun today either," Bess agreed. "I think I deserve it after yesterday. Now I know where the expression 'scared to death' comes from. I honestly believed I was going to die of fright before those thugs even did anything to me."

Nancy leaned over and tugged on Bess's blond hair. "I know. It was a nightmare. But it's all over."

"Is it?" Bess punched her pillow, her expression sober. "Maybe for you, but I've got some serious thinking to do."

"Alan?" Nancy asked softly.

Bess nodded. "He told lies to get what he wanted. I didn't realize the boy I fell in love with would do something like that."

George pulled a chair up next to the bed. "But he also saved our lives. Bess, your boyfriend's a hero."

"Maybe."

"Barton and Roger sure seem to think so," Nancy put in. "They wouldn't have offered to help him out otherwise."

"Yeah, just think of it, Bess. He might get his dream one day, after all," George remarked.

"I'm thinking of it. But I'm also thinking that I want to take it more slowly with him. What happened made me realize that there's a lot about Alan Wales I don't know."

"But you still feel something for him, don't you?" Nancy asked.

"Well, when the chemistry's right . . ." Bess's round face grew pink.

"Good. Because I told Mrs. Chen to seat you two next to each other," Nancy said with a laugh. "Oh, did I tell you that my dad's bringing Ann Nordquist to the luncheon?"

George's brown eyes opened wide. "Talk about chemistry!"

"Yeah. Dad's really enjoying her company." Nancy sighed. "I can't tell you how glad I am to have a suspect turn out innocent."

"And speaking of couples," George said, giving Nancy a poke, "how are you and Ned doing?"

"I think we're going to be all right." Nancy smiled brightly. "As a matter of fact, this afternoon he's taking me on a very special boat ride to a tiny island!" She raised her eyebrows suggestively. "It's a start."

"Sounds romantic," Bess sighed.

Nancy giggled. "Yeah, it's called the ferry to the Statue of Liberty! Now how about getting up,

Bess, or the guests of honor are going to miss their own luncheon."

"And don't take too long putting on your makeup," George added.

"Okay, okay." Bess climbed out of bed. "Are Barton and Roger and all the Fenders going to be there?"

"Absolutely," Nancy replied. "Hey, did you know that Barton told me he's going to write a song about us and the whole mystery? He's going to call it 'Scared to Death.'"

"Wow! You mean every time we turn on our radios in River Heights we're going to hear about ourselves?" Bess asked.

"An instant souvenir," Nancy answered.

"Maybe they'll even make it into a video," George said hopefully.

"That would be neat," Nancy agreed. "And I know just the threesome to play the detective and her two friends. . . ."

Nancy Drew
Mystery Stories

Nancy Drew is the best-known and most-loved girl detective ever. Join her and her best friends, George Fayne and Bess Marvin, in her many thrilling adventures available in Armada.

The Chalet School Series
Elinor M. Brent-Dyer

Elinor M. Brent-Dyer has written many books about life at the famous alpine school. Follow the thrilling adventures of Joey, Mary-Lou and all the other well-loved characters in these delightful stories, available only in Armada.